Savannah of Williamsburg

Being the Account of a Young London Squirrel
Virginia 1705

by
Jennifer Susannah Devore

D1114253

Tall Cotton, Inc.
Williamsburg, Virginia

Savannah of Williamsburg: Being the Account of a Young London Squirrel Virginia 1705

Tall Cotton, Inc.
119 Hempstead Road
Williamsburg, Virginia 23187

savannahsquirrel@yahoo.com

Cover photo and author photo by Gary David Devore
Cover design by Jennifer Susannah Devore and Gary David Devore
Manufactured and printed in the United States of America

For individual, bulk and school-discount ordering, please contact:
Tall Cotton, Inc.
savannahsquirrel@yahoo.com

Library of Congress Data: TX 6-085-275
Second Edition 2005

For Dante

What a we-weef!

Chapter 1

Savannah's teeth had begun to smart. As posh and lovely as
her carriage was, the unpaved road to Williamsburg was
dreadfully rough. There were potholes, mud puddles,
intermittent rocks and as she peered up from her seat on the
fine, red velvet bench and out the carriage window, rain
seemed unavoidable. However, Miss Savannah Squirrel
was far too excited to be truly irritated by the carriage ride.
She was going to the capital of the British colony known as
Virginia: the great capital city called Williamsburg!

Just three months before, Savannah sailed across the
Atlantic from London for Virginia. Gossip circulated
throughout her network of friends and community
acquaintances that she was so brassy, so unladylike as to
sail across the Atlantic to America on her own. This was
not what a young lady squirrel of fine breeding did at the
turn of the 18th Century. Nevertheless, Savannah had
explorer in her fine blood and knew she must discover this
Virginia, even if no one else she knew would. Oh, the trials
she endured on that great ship. The scarcity of food (When
the humans have not enough nourishment, there are
certainly no crumbs for a squirrel.), the long days without
fresh water and the stench! Oh, my! The stench! For a

refined and proper young lady such as Miss Savannah Squirrel, such discomfort was nearly an impossible ordeal. She endured, though, for she knew exactly what awaited her across the sea: the unknown! America was rumored to be a land of wide, open spaces, numerous rivers, and many trees! So many trees!

As the carriage continued to bounce along the main route through Charles City County into Williamsburg, the road ran parallel between the James River and the York River, a waterway that fed into the Chesapeake Bay and was home to many a plantation and farm. Because the James River provided access to so many ports and cities along the Eastern shoreline, gentleman farmers and planters selected home sites along its sylvan riverbanks. If one sailed down the James, one would see spectacular manses along its edge. Savannah planned to sail the river as soon as she was settled in her new home and had some free time for herself. She had seen a great deal of it as her ship, The Grand Anne, sailed into Jamestown. The trees were too bountiful to count. At night, the sounds of strange creatures could be heard and, even at the height of day, the forests were so thick, only black could be seen. Savannah thought a tour of the river's edge might be better in the daylight. She was a very small animal and knew not to be wandering about, out of doors, at night. With that thought in mind, she looked out the window of her carriage and noticed the daylight beginning to fade presently. Looking into the darkening forests on either side of the road, she was very happy to be inside a safe carriage.

Every once in a while, a long stretch of land rolled past the carriage window: bare of trees but thick with people, collectively bent at the waist, in clusters like beds of mussels at low tide. The light wind rustled quietly through the reed shade of the window, rolled up enough to allow her to see, but not so much as to allow entry of the chilled air. Occasionally, a field of young wheat rolled past, the wee stalks bent wistfully in unison, as if all leaning to hear the same secret. There was little cover from the chilly spring air for the small population of slaves working those fields, providing the necessary means to maintain the magnificent brick homes that loomed over the fields in the distance, like great brick and clay foremen, ensuring work continued until nightfall.

Trying to take her mind off the strong feelings she had about slavery, something she was unaccustomed to in London, and also, trying to push out of her vivid imagination the unknown animals out there in the too near distance, she smoothed her French-blue, silk polonaise skirt and lay back against her Turkish carpet bag to take a wee nap. She closed her eyes and tried to recall the first glimpse she'd ever had of the Virginia coastline from the sea.

The seas seemed endless as she watched from her hiding spot in the captain's quarter. She peered out the leaded windows for days upon days. Each morning, hungry and never well rested, she looked out the window, over the ocean and thought, "Today?". The continuous motion of the great ship and the wretched smells of too many people in too small a place for too many days had made her very ill. Her wee food supply had run out long before they reached shore and the occasional morsel she did find was either rotten or not nearly enough to satisfy her tummy. Many of the people on the ship were chronically ill or, sadly, died. It was not an easy journey. Numbering better than sixty days on the sea, there were people who perished from hunger, disease or infection. Savannah had been famished, but other than that, her journey was endurable. She felt nauseous from all the offensive smells and the motion sickness, but she always knew she would be well as soon as they found land. Her biggest problem during those two months was Petruchio, a large and brutal mastiff on board.

One of the captain's personal guests was a Sir Roland Grahame. He was sailing to Virginia to serve as a councilor to the Royal Governor Edward Nott. He was very cruel to the steerage passengers and frequently allowed his pet dog, Petruchio to corner the peasants and scare them for hours on end. Petruchio appeared to have enjoyed this game, barking and barking non-stop. That is, until he had gotten whiff of Savannah. He knew there was a squirrel on board and was determined to find her and, from what Savannah surmised, to make her into a nice snack. Besides being mean, Petruchio was a snob. He used his great size to intimidate everyone on the ship and he refused to eat anything except the best steaks, and Sir Roland obliged him. While the rest of the ship was starving, Sir Roland fed wonderful meals to Petruchio, who left half of it behind. Just to be insidious, Sir Roland would then take Petruchio's leftovers on deck and throw them overboard, in full view of the starving passengers. Once in a while, Savannah had been able to sneak a tidbit before Sir Grahame confiscated the leftovers; this is what had first alerted Petruchio to her presence. Normally, she would have been smarter than that, but she was so hungry, she had no other option. She had successfully evaded Petruchio the entire trip and was happy to never see that cumbersome beast ever again.

This transatlantic route and The Grand Anne had been sailed a number of times before, so Savannah had confidence in the captain, his ship and his crew. In her makeshift sleeping quarters beneath the captain's bunk, she tried to imagine what it would have been like two-hundred years ago in the late 15th or early 16th Century, to have been one of the first explorers to sail for unknown lands: Cortez, Columbus, Magellan. Not knowing when or if land would ever appear must have been terrifying. Luckily, this captain knew the route well. Having stashed herself away in his cabin, she was able to listen in on a number of important meetings. The most exciting she had heard was one in which the captain revealed he expected to reach land the next morning. That night, she couldn't sleep a wink and waited eagerly for the great cry of, "Land Ho!". When she finally heard the crow's nest sailor declare those words, she ran to the small, round window and waited. Obviously, being higher than everyone else, the crow's nest sailor saw the land first. She had to wait a little while. Yet, when she saw it for the first time, she was stunned. As the land grew closer and closer, it made her little heart skip a beat. So many trees she'd never seen! After all, she was a city squirrel: London-born and -bred. She'd heard the tales of acres and acres of trees, but she'd never imagined it to be like this! She knew she could build a new home in any one of them and it would be perfect, as long as the night didn't turn too scary.

Again, bouncing along in the carriage, she tried to detach herself from thoughts of the mysterious and ominous Virginia nights that continued to sneak into her subconscious. Looking pensively at an abandoned field, stalks naked and stripped, dancing like skeletons in the late sun, she thought about London, instead. Savannah sighed. She missed London: the theatre, the ballet, her French lessons and violin instruction. Alas, the noise, the smell and the ever-present danger of all those carriages near her fine, bushy tail were all too much worry for such a very small animal. At a music salon one evening, she had overheard talk of a ship sailing for Virginia. Savannah decided it was her time to grow. That night, she had packed her most valuable items, including her violin and books, set out her finest polonaise and ribbons and readied herself for the two-month sail to America.

Her French instructress, Madame Squires, and her violin maestro, Mr. Cunningham bid her farewell with a small gathering and care packages of acorn spread, mulberry preserves and fresh apple juice. Savannah was concerned she might not find suitable tutors such as these in Virginia. Her mother, though wanting her daughter to stay, assured her that the colony was growing and drawing in men of great upbringing and education. She would be able to find instruction appropriate to her levels. Why, there was even a college there now that had been chartered by the late King William and Queen Mary. Savannah's mother, father and baby sister had cried terribly when she boarded the ship. Nonetheless, they knew she had to follow her dream and were happy for their young Savannah and her new life in America.

"B-b-b-bump!!! Slam!" A ridiculously large pothole jolted Savannah back to the present. She wiped a teeny tear from her eye and looked out the window. Rain clouds seemed to be hanging in the sky, full, just waiting for the order to empty.

"My goodness!", she thought to herself. "I will certainly need a fine, stuffed pillow and a pot of hot, peppermint tea when we finally arrive. This seems to me at the moment worse than the crossing."

The road was particularly rough. She was accustomed to the relatively well-traveled roads of London. There, so many people traversed the main routes that had been in place for so long, the roads had been smoothed and paved by years and years of carriage wheels, foot traffic and horses' hooves. Here though, the roads were somewhat newer and infrequently traveled, at least in comparison to London. It all made for a horribly uncomfortable ride. Still looking out at the vast wilderness, it seemed so untouched and worth the efforts. Savannah's flounces and crinolines rustled as she rubbed her hindquarter with a gloved paw. Sitting up straight, hunger occurred to her. She tightened her cloak around her shoulders and pulled around her carpetbag, rummaging about inside, and looking for a nibble.

"Hmm," she mumbled as she rummaged through her bag. "Aha! This shall suffice until we reach town."

Savannah pulled from her bag a medium-sized walnut half and a small acorn top of raspberry jam for dipping. Next, she pulled off her gloves so as not to muss them. Contentedly, albeit jostled, she broke apart small pieces of walnut meat and dipped them in the jam. She did this in a most ladylike fashion and dropped not a bit on her delicate silk bodice.

"Savannah, dear?" a polished voice, tinged with both Virginian and English influences, queried from above, "There remains only one more quarter hour and we shall be in Her Majesty's capital of Williamsburg. Gather your belongings and ready yourself."

Savannah peered upwards, cheeks full of delicious walnut, and smiled at her handsome and bewigged friend in compliance. Col. William Byrd II was Savannah's best friend in Virginia. Col. Byrd, as she properly addressed him, was a refined and distinguished Virginia gentleman who had just recently inherited the marvelous family estate from his father, Col. William Byrd I. The family property was called Westover and sat upon the James River. His father had purchased it from a Mr. Theodorick Bland back in 1688. Now that his mother, Mary Horsmanden, and his father had passed away, and being the only son in a family of four children, Westover was now his property. It was a stunning plantation about five hours outside of Williamsburg.

When Savannah first arrived in Virginia a couple of months ago, she took up residence in a grand old oak tree on the Westover grounds. She and Col. Byrd had met one sunny day whilst both were out exploring the property. They had shared some nuts and cider and discussed the importance and reputation of Colonial Williamsburg as a representative of England's crown. They had also discovered they had mutual interests in discussing western philosophy, the arts and though not his favorite subject, international commerce. True, ladies were not generally encouraged to discuss politics, trade or any other matter of business, yet they were alone, amongst the trees, and Savannah was quite intelligent and made for a worthy conversationalist. Before they realized, the sun had descended and they had become fast friends.

Up until just this year, William Byrd II served as a colonial agent from Virginia to London. For the past eight years, he also served as a representative of the Virginia Assembly. He had now returned to Virginia to serve a royal appointment as Receiver-General. William was from a very distinguished and important family. His father had been a wealthy plantation owner whom had made a fortune in Indian trade. His uncle, William's great-uncle, had been appointed to the King's Council in the House of Burgesses back in the 1670s. William's mother, Mary Horsmanden, was a member of the Virginia social elite with a grandfather tied to the Royalist Army. This grandfather had fled England after Parliament's execution of Charles I. The ill-fated king's loyalists had no place in England in the 1650s when Oliver Cromwell changed it from a monarchy to a republic.

During their childhood, Mary provided William and his sisters with the social status needed to progress at this time in Virginia. This connection was Green Springs mansion: home to Governor and Mrs. William Berkley and first mansion ever to be built in Virginia. William felt the power that surrounded Green Springs whenever they visited. It was the absolute height of nobility for Virginia's landed-class and William knew he wanted to remain part of that class throughout his life.

Savannah thought about all of this and felt rather fortunate to know someone of such import. Of course, she would have liked him no matter what his social standing was; she just thought he was nice.

Thinking about Virginia's elite and the ruling-class, her mind wandered to government and she remembered something William had told her about a great new capitol building that would house the new government. Since the capital city had been moved from Jamestown to Williamsburg a few years back, it was very important to have a new and prestigious building. Col. Byrd had invited Savannah to accompany him on his journey and to stay with him while in the capital. She had accepted gracefully and eagerly.

Savannah tucked away the remainder of her snacks and tidied herself. She fluffed her powdered wig and brushed the crumbs from her skirt. She put on her gloves and tugged down on her bodice so as to ensure its neat and unwrinkled appearance and grimaced at the uncomfortable whalebone-fragment stays that bound her. Fashion! Hmph! She looked up at William who was doing the same. He brushed off his frock coat, re-extended the lace ruffles from under his great cuffs, brushed the dust from his polished, black, leather, jack boots with a silk handkerchief, patted his full-bottomed wig to release any road debris and re-tied his two front hair ribbons. Not only did Col. William Byrd II's professional life include posts as a colonial diplomat to London, an Assembly representative, and now as Receiver-General, but also personally, he was known as a man of fashion, a dandy if you will. The height of English mode was actually the height of French mode, thanks to King Louis XIV and his *menus des plaisirs*: members of his court. Indeed, he was known throughout Virginia to be "the colony's most polished gentleman". Savannah admired her friend as he prepared to exit the coach. Savannah sighed deeply and felt nothing but the dearest kind of friendship for her distinguished companion. Suddenly, the coach jerked to a stop and threw Savannah into William's leather encased shin. He picked her up gently, brushed off her skirt and replaced some disheveled curls.

"Are you hurt, my dear girl?", he asked sincerely.

"Thank you, but of course not! Lead me to the Capitol!"

As ladylike and genteel as Miss Savannah was, she was as self-assured and resilient. William chuckled to himself so as not to insult the proud, cosmopolitan squirrel.

"As you desire, Milady."

With that, he opened his carpetbag and in it gingerly placed Savannah's teeny carpetbag. Next, he made a cushy spot of some silk handkerchiefs in which Savannah could sit.

"Your second carriage awaits, Mademoiselle.", William gestured for Savannah to hop in the bag.

"I do hope this ride is more pleasurable than the last.", she commented with a smile as she rubbed her bottom again.

With a wink and a smile, William closed his bag without latching it so Savannah could peek out and breathe. The coachman opened the carriage door just as Savannah popped her head down inside the bag.

"Your bag, Sir ?", the footman asked.

"Thank you, good man. However, I should prefer to carry it personally.", William loosely secured the bag under his arm.

"Very well, Sir. I shall water and stable the horses and then situate your belongings at Mrs. Pritchen's tavern. Should you be requiring my services before dinner, Sir?"

"No. Please tell Mrs. Pritchen I will be in shortly after a walk to stretch my legs."

"Very good, Sir."

William's footman mounted his seat on top of the carriage and drove down the main street to a nearby stable. As the coach rolled away, a somewhat unexpected sight rolled into view.

"Savannah,", he whispered toward his bag, "come out from hiding. No one is about and I would like your opinion of your first glimpse of Williamsburg."

Savannah rustled about inside the bag and slowly opened it from within. First, her powdered white curls appeared, followed by the French-blue ribbon set within them. Under that, Savannah's soft and sleek, furry face peered out from the carpet bag, her big, brown eyes as wide and sparkling as two smoky topazes. Her plump cheeks and long whiskers twitched with curiosity.

"Oh, my", she worried, "it's not very palatial, is it? I mean, should not it resemble, perhaps Versailles? I mean, this is a direct representation of our good Queen Anne, is it not?"

Savannah wrinkled her nose and surveyed the long, sparse road. She could only make out a couple of large brick buildings, a few smaller buildings of white and red clapboard, plenty of trees, which did please her, and a moderate population. Actually, what she saw were more animals than people. Horses were tied up outside taverns and shops while sheep, pigs, goats and chickens ran freely about town. Dogs and cats were also well represented. Most humans she saw, hustling about trying to avoid remnants left behind by the livestock, were attired mostly in common, utilitarian, drab clothing. With a raised eyebrow and gloved hand upon her tiny hip, she looked up at William and awaited an explanation.

Chapter II

Savannah worked herself and her great flounces of silk up from the depths of William's bag. Looking about to make sure no one was looking, she scurried up his wide cuff, tripped on a large, covered button and continued up his arm until she settled on his shoulder. William looked around also, confident no one could see Savannah on his shoulder. Not that he didn't care deeply for Savannah, but he did have a reputation to uphold. It was very uncommon for gentlemen in the Queen's service to be talking to squirrels. There were two reasons for this: one was that people didn't talk to animals; two was that squirrels were a commercial enemy of gentlemen farmers and planters. Being a city squirrel, Savannah wasn't aware of this; however, here in America, tobacco and, to a lesser degree, other crops were the livelihoods of Virginia colonists. Without the money the crops brought, there would be no clothing, no food, no anything. Savannah wasn't interested in destroying their crops; she abhorred tobacco and as far as something like wheat went, she wouldn't know what to do with a stalk if it jumped in her lap. Still, they didn't know that. They assumed all squirrels were the same and all squirrels were problematic.

"Once they get to know me they shall come to understand I am their friend and would do nothing to destroy their industry.", she had explained to William during the carriage ride.

"They will not understand. All they shall see is your fluffy tail and grey fur and shall not give you a moment to explain yourself, but bump you down the road with their highly polished boots. For now, it is best if we keep things quiet.", William said.

Savannah didn't agree with such nonsense, but she did understand she was a stranger and a guest and, for now, would oblige William's request. She turned her attention toward the sparse town and awaited an explanation as to its simplicity. Answering Savannah's question about the small nature of the town, William explained.

"Williamsburg is indeed very humble, yet quietly commanding. It is merely the beginning my dear girl." William Byrd II stood on the roadway and looked east, far down the main street. "Look, Savannah, far, far down the road sits our Capitol building."
Savannah turned her bewigged head, wrinkled her wee nose and squinted, stretching her neck out as far as it would go. With some effort, she saw the smallish, odd-shaped, brick building.

"That's our Capitol?", she asked uncertainly.

"That is our Capitol and that is where I shall be working from time to time in my duties as Receiver-General."

"Then what is that structure over there?", Savannah switched her head back to the left, looking west this time.

"Why that is the College.", he explained.

The college! Schooling! Savannah had heard of this institution. It was certainly no Oxford, but she was in Virginia and would embrace all that was Virginian.

"The College of King William and Queen Mary?!"

"The one and only.", stated William. "Except we call it the College. I know you've missed your tutoring; perhaps we can find you some private instruction here from some of the more open-minded faculty,", he offered, "some who are not prejudiced against squirrels.", he added with a wink.

"Oh, I do hope so!" Savannah clapped her tiny-gloved paws together. "I would like to continue my French studies and my violin, but I should also like to begin a course of study that includes some philosophy, Latin and maybe even law! Of course, it does look a tad small for a university. I have visited Oxford and Cambridge and they are indeed grand."

"Well, Savannah, someday our school will be quite grand, as well. However, it only received its charter in 1693, fully completed just ten years ago in 1695. Give it time my young scholar."

Savannah nodded in comprehension, a bit ashamed at her snobbery. Then, she tilted her head to the right and pondered something. William picked up his bag and invited Savannah to hop in for a walk down the street.

William walked along the main thoroughfare as Savannah sat upon the pile of handkerchiefs in his bag and spied the sights. Over the crunching of rocks, leaves and dirt under William's boots, Savannah heard the sounds of an early 18th Century town. She heard children playing and giggling, bells ringing, adults talking in low conversational tones, babies crying, and the clip-clop of hooves combined with the grating of wood over gravel as carriages, both fine and menial rolled by the two friends. Then, she heard a sound that was terribly familiar. It was low, rumbling and very unfriendly. She looked all around and as the noise grew thicker she ducked down into the bag. Searching the faces of passers-by for reactions, she noticed no one else reacted to this noise. Why did she find it so unnerving? She knew one thing, and that was there is fear in ignorance. If she hid from the noise, she would never be able to face it and therefore deal with it logically. She looked through the opening of the bag at William. He seemed happy and completely unaffected by the great noise. There it was again. It came and went in short blurbs of sound. She had to face her fear, well, at least look at it from a safe distance. She poked out her head slowly from the bag and looked around carefully. Her eyebrows were wrinkled in apprehension and William noticed this.

"Savannah, what seems to be troubling you?"

Surprised he had noticed, she told him of the frightening noise. Then, in the midst of explanation, it came to her. She knew what the noise was! Quickly, she ducked back into the bag. William was surprised by her fear.

"What is it?", he asked worriedly as he surveyed the area. Slowly protruding from the bag again, she looked in the direction of the sound.

"Woof, Woof, Woof!", it resounded in deep, booming beats.

She focused on the noise with her eyes and found the source. There he was: Petruchio. Savannah had instant recollections of almost being discovered on the ship. Her breathing became faster and faster. She thought she had gotten over the fear after she left the ship, but now she had all new fears, and not just for her own safety. Things were going so well with William, she couldn't stand it if her presence made things difficult for her new friend. How would he explain a crop sacker in his bag?

Standing next to his master, that horrible Sir Roland Grahame, Petruchio slobbered profusely all over the ridiculous lace ruffle Sir Roland had tied around Petruchio's neck. Visually following the tacky, diamond leash, she saw Sir Roland was rather ridiculous himself. He sported a shocking-pink frock coat with the largest cuffs she'd ever seen, even in London; on his coat and cuffs were gold buttons the size of teacup saucers. His ruffles were so long that he kept catching them on the gold buttons of his breeches. He carried a tall walking stick topped with what looked like a giant ruby. He wore shiny, black shoes so high that he tippled and toppled even as he stood still. Diamond buckles on those shoes made Savannah's eyes smart as the fading sun caught their facets, making a blinding glint. His wig was a whole other problem. The top half stood about two feet high and was white as snow. The bottom half was tied into three sections with matching pink bows that were tied very low. Still, with all this, Savannah thought his makeup to be the silliest. Sure, gentlemen wore makeup, just as William did on many an evening for gatherings or parties, yet not to this degree in the daytime.

Sir Grahame, however, wore red lipstick and two perfectly placed party patches: fake, black moles that he drew on his face, one over his lips and one on his cheek. His face was powdered so thickly white that she wondered if it would melt should he stand too close to a candle. Upon that, he had drawn two dramatic swaths of bright rouge on his rather round and fleshy cheeks. Savannah wondered if he was storing nuts in there. As Savannah was laughing inside at Sir Grahame's excessive wardrobe, William very subtly spoke into the bag, so no one would be curious.

"Worry yourself not about Petruchio, I know him and his master Sir Grahame well."

"You know that beast? He was a menace to me all the way here and that Sir Grahame is a horrible man. He threw away perfectly good food on the ship, right in front of all the hungry passengers."

"That sounds like Rolly. Sir Roland Grahame's family and mine have been acquaintances for generations. He and I have been members of the Royal Society since 1696. We share a mutual friendship with Sir Robert Southwell: our mutual sponsor upon election into the Society. Unfortunately, we have been and remain socially tied rather tightly. In truth, he has never been kind to a single person for as long as I can remember. We were classmates at Felsted Grammar School back in England. As children, he would play tricks on me every chance he had.", William recalled.

Savannah was amazed at the coincidence that they would both know Petruchio and his master. She laughed when he called him Rolly. This made him seem far less menacing. However, William assured her, be not fooled. He was indeed malicious to the core.

"He uses Petruchio to frighten and intimidate people into doing his bidding. He owns hundreds of slaves and is inhumane to every one of them.", William said morosely. "Sometimes, he even punishes them by sending Petruchio to attack them. Some have even died from these attacks."

Savannah really was scared, now. She looked over at Petruchio and couldn't help but focus on his long, sharp, yellow teeth ensconced in a veil of, most likely very smelly, drool.

"What is he doing in Williamsburg?", Savannah asked very worriedly.

"Rolly has been appointed to the Governor's Council in the House of Burgesses."

"You mean you have to work with him?"

"On occasion, yes. That also means that Petruchio will be a regular presence. We shall have to be very careful,

Savannah. Neither Rolly nor Petruchio can find out about you."

Savannah agreed and they decided it was a good time to head down the main street to the tavern where they would be lodging.

Just as William had loosely closed the bag on Savannah and they had begun walking toward the tavern of kind Mrs. Pritchen, Sir Roland Grahame recognized William and flagged a loud and very irritating screech with his lace handkerchief, "Hellooo, Col. Byrd! Hold there a moment!"

Rolly finished his current conversation and sashayed across the street, Petruchio prancing haughtily by his side, his diamond leash and collar sparkling in the bright, evening sunset. Savannah was terrified and kicked William's leg through the bag. William understood this kick to mean he should close the bag securely. He nonchalantly locked the bag shut and offered a deep bow, one leg extended, to Sir Rolly. He hated doing this, but Rolly was Sir Roland Grahame, whereas William was not a "Sir" himself. This meant that Rolly was slightly above him in the pecking order of English society. So, he bowed and smiled, grating his teeth.

"Hello, Sir Grahame. How wonderful to see you. I had not expected to see you until sessions begin next month."

"Yes, but you know how difficult it is to set up the plantation after being in London for a while. The house is in complete disorder. Those stupid slaves did nothing while I was gone. Really, the incompetence has made it very difficult for me; when I need someone to brush my wig or clip my toenails, they are off doing work that should have been done ages ago. But that is okay,", he said coldly as he patted Petruchio on the head, who had become very interested in William's bag, "Petruchio has been helping me with the, how shall we say, discipline. Have you not, Petruchio?"

Petruchio licked his chops, barked a deafening "Yes!", and returned to William's bag. Without drawing too much attention, William kept pushing Petruchio away with his boot and switched the bag back and forth from hand to hand. Inside the bag, Savannah was curled up in one corner, arms clutched around her knees, and fantasized about jumping out of the bag and taking care of Petruchio herself. However, size and William's reputation would not allow such action. So she sat and waited to hear the two councilors bid farewells.

In short time, Sir Rolly and William said their good-byes and agreed to meet for dinner on one of the coming evenings. Sir Rolly had a hard time dragging Petruchio away from the bag. Sir Rolly eyed the bag suspiciously. William just said, "Sausage.". When the coast was clear, William unclasped the bag and Savannah emerged with trepidation.

"Why I should clearly give that great beast a swift kick in the nose!", Savannah declared, all fear now gone as Petruchio was out of sight.

"Violence is no way to handle a situation, Savannah", William admonished.

Savannah was ashamed of herself for being so emotional and unthinking. She knew that kicking and hitting would only cause more problems and make her no better than Petruchio. She decided then and there that she would do her best to ignore Petruchio. She didn't have the time to hate anybody. She was beginning a new life of education, friendship and philosophical importance. If she hated someone, that meant she was wasting time thinking about them when she should be thinking about politics, law and mathematics. Petruchio would become a non-subject, she told herself.

Having made this decision, her original thought occurred to her. Something bothered her when she and William first began walking the main street and the whole Sir Rolly and Petruchio issue had sidetracked her curiosity.

"Col. Byrd, I wanted to ask you something about the town.", she told him.

"I guess our discussions were interrupted. Please, ask anything you like."

He noticed the sun was setting fast and thought it safe to place Savannah back on his shoulder. He did so and she took a moment to look around the darkening streets. Those Virginia trees were becoming darker and scarier out there beyond the buildings. She hoped she could find a lovely tree closer to town. She was thinking about owls and the possible danger they could pose when William suspended her thoughts.

"What did you wish to ask, Miss Savannah?"

"Oh, yes.", she remembered. "I was just thinking that as simple, yet majestic as the buildings are here in Williamsburg, I see only three very noticeable ones, not including the few shops and taverns."

"Mm-hmm.", listened William intently.

"It seems to me that visitors might not think Williamsburg very, well,", she stammered for just the right word, careful not to insult, "worthy of a capital city. I mean, it is charming, in a very provincial way. Nevertheless, it is not very bustling, like London or Paris or Vienna.", Savannah explained her concern.

"Understandable thought. However, may I introduce an idea?", he offered.

"Of course.", Savannah turned the conversation over to her knowledgeable friend.

William set his bag and then himself on a wooden bench about halfway down the thoroughfare between the College and the Capitol. He looked at the sky, which was quickly turning to night; thinking it very peaceful and extremely quiet. This was a nice ending to a day of rough travel and unexpected meetings. Savannah eagerly awaited William's explanation. He was so enlightened, she knew whatever view he had would be very informative.

"You see, Savannah, a city must implement certain elements at its center in order to establish itself as a capital. These elements, in turn, help the city to feed on itself and draw in more people, more business and thus, more wealth. It grows upon itself. Williamsburg is in its very early stages. I know you understand a mere six years ago we were not even a capital city. That was Jamestown. In fact, this town was not even called Williamsburg. It was known as Middle Plantation."

"Why was it called that? Why did someone change the name?", a baffled Savannah politely demanded, intent on proper answers.

"It was named Middle Plantation because of its position in the middle of the James and York Rivers."

"I see, a middle ground. It is a beautiful name, why change it?"

"When too many fires, too many mosquitoes, too much disease and too many Indian attacks plagued our old Jamestown capital, some leading men in the government moved to move the capital here. While Middle Plantation was a very lovely and descriptive name, it did not properly represent the British crown. So, it was thus named for our beloved King William, William's town, to be specific. In fact it is safer, drier, prettier and closer to some of our leading men's homes on the rivers."

Savannah thought about all of this new information for a moment. After some pondering, she decided it all made sense and she stated, "That makes sense."

"Now, my dear curious squirrel,", William addressed his companion, " if you have the time early tomorrow morning, we shall further discuss the concept of

Williamsburg building upon itself. We will begin a tour of the town and the three, primary foundations you noticed when we first arrived. Those three buildings will, by their very existence and usage, give way to a greater population of citizens. We shall visit the College of William and Mary, the Capitol, and Bruton Parish Church. Right now, though, we should go directly to Mrs. Pritchen's tavern. She is expecting us and most likely has a delicious, hot dinner ready for us."

"Mmmm", she thought.

A hot serving of yams or crab cakes sounded very tasty. With such a busy day, she only just now realized that the walnuts and jam she had nibbled in the carriage were not enough food for a growing squirrel. Savannah jumped off the bench and into William's bag. She straightened her wig, checked her ruffles and bows to be straight and extended to William one wee, gloved paw. William offered his larger, gloved hand and they shook in agreement. "Tomorrow, we shall talk of the future."

Chapter III

The morning air in the house was chilly, yet pleasant: the kind of chilly that makes you want to stay in bed but has already enlivened all your senses. As Savannah looked at the bare room around her, she noticed that William was gone. She listened for a moment and heard his voice downstairs, chatting with their tavern hostess, Mrs. Pritchen. Hearing the *clanks* and *clunks* of pottery and silver, she assumed Mrs. Pritchen was making breakfast. Shivering a little, Savannah thought of cocoa. It sounded perfect for such a morning and she hoped there might be a mug of it awaiting her at the table. The smell of eggs and biscuits crept up the stairs, mingling with the tasty smells of unknown cakes and this hurried her along. She was very hungry, even after last night's dinner of clam chowder and crab cakes. Thinking about last night recalled what could have been a disaster. Luckily, in the end, Mrs. Pritchen was not upset about Savannah.

Last night, without thinking, Savannah had ventured into the kitchen to introduce herself to Dante, Mrs. Pritchen's cat. When she first saw Dante that night in the garden, she was very excited at the prospect of another new friend. Savannah always got on very well with cats and was anxious to meet this Dante. In fact, Dante was quite happy to see a new face scuttling across the kitchen floor, waving her hanky. Mrs. Pritchen was not. She was horrified to see a squirrel in her kitchen. Screaming and shooing Savannah out the back door with a broom, Savannah found herself very insulted. Obviously, Mrs. Pritchen didn't know Savannah was a well-heeled, worldly, educated squirrel.

William emerged from the parlor where he had been engaged in some pre-supping Shakespeare. Hearing the ruckus, he ran to the kitchen, took the broom from Mrs. Pritchen and sat her down at the kitchen table, calming her with the temptation of a nice cup of tea. He explained Savannah and their situation to her. He also explained the need for discretion with regards to her presence. Dante also listened, thinking Savannah very interesting, having been from London and all. Once all was clear, Mrs. Pritchen said she quite understood and had no intention of telling their secret.

"If truth be known,", she confided, "I had a secret friend who was a fox. This was up in Massachusetts. Nobody could know because foxes were often killed and used as wraps for ladies' necks."

Savannah shivered at the thought of such horror.

"He lived with me for a long time until I moved down here.", she finished her story.

"What happened to him?", Savannah asked with great concern.

"He is very well, my dear. Bertram stayed on my property and the new owners became his good friends.", she assured Savannah.

Savannah liked happy endings. Considering everything, it seemed all would be happy here, too. Mrs. Pritchen seemed to easily take to Savannah; and, Dante, the sleek tabby, had given her all the animal news of the town as they sipped tea before bed last night. During their late-night discourse, Savannah wanted to share her story of Petruchio, but saw no reason to give Dante nightmares. So she waited.

She crawled out of the warm, little bed William made for her just under his bed. The wee, wool blanket was plenty warm if she wrapped her tail around it just so. Even though she had seen daffodils beginning to bloom in town, it was still quite cold this time of year. Reluctantly, she unwrapped her tail. Taking a deep breath, she threw off the blanket, sat erect and placed her bare paws on the cold, wooden floor. She jumped up from the shock and suddenly found herself standing and wide-awake.

Opening her steamer trunk, she tried to decide what to wear. Savannah was very excited about today's events: touring about town with her gracious friend Col. Byrd. Considering the day's probable weather, Savannah chose a burgundy, damask gown with an embroidered, floral bodice. She topped it with a hooded cloak of matching, burgundy, wool broadcloth. Because she anticipated not spending the entire day snuggled warmly in William's bag, she also wore a pair of knitted, silk stockings in a dark gold and some brocaded slippers in the same color with jeweled buckles. Her gloves were a pair of printed leather she had received as a gift from Paris. On the back of each hand, was a design of small dancing squirrel. Savannah also chose a taffeta bonnet of dark gold. She checked herself in her tiny hand mirror, fluffed up her cheeks and went below stairs to breakfast. As she descended the stairs, the delicious smell of hot cocoa wafted through her little, brown, squirrel nose.

The dining table was set beautifully but very simply. Everyone had a place setting of pottery bowls, plates and mugs. There were silver forks and knives and a lovely, blue pitcher of fresh cow's milk. Patiently, Savannah waited for the hot cocoa, which came just after Mrs. Pritchen finished serving the eggs and huge slices of Virginia ham to both Col. Byrd and Dante. Savannah was happy with her mug of cocoa and small serving of last night's chowder with a side of eggs. Breakfast was not as leisurely as last night's dinner, but that's because everyone had a lot of work to do. Mrs. Pritchen had to get to the market square early enough to get the freshest meats, cheeses and fish. William and Savannah had a lot of ground to cover in their day of touring and even Dante had work to do. Dante's job was to be sure the garden stayed free of any and all bugs that might destroy some of the garden vegetables. (Dante was a great hunter of flies and beetles, putting his favorite sword to good use.) After that, Dante had some relatives to visit behind the Bruton Parish graveyard and then down to the College to visit a sick mouse friend. On the way, he had to pick some flowers to take to Bartholomew, his mouse friend.

After breakfast was finished, William took some time for himself in the salon. Ritually, but usually before breakfast, William took each morning to read his Greek and Hebrew verses. This morning, after yesterday's long journey, he slept too late and was forced to delay his readings until after breakfast. Mrs. Pritchen ran a strict table, expecting everyone who was in the house to be at the table with everyone else at the same time. After he was finished reading his verses, he called Savannah to the kitchen, cleared the table and pulled out a map of the town. It wasn't very detailed, because there were only a few buildings, but he wanted Savannah to have an overall idea of where everything was in relation to Mrs. Pritchen's house, in case Savannah got lost.

"If you will notice on the map I have drawn for you, you shall see we are very close to the Capitol. Actually, when we walk outside, you should be able to look just to the right and see it.", he pointed to an amateur drawing of a building on the map. "We are here, on the south side of the Main Street, which runs west to east. The College of William and Mary lies at the farthest west end and the Capitol lies at the farthest east end. Bruton Parish Church is almost in the middle, but a little closer to the College than the Capitol." Savannah hopped up on the table and walked the distance of Main Street, stopping at each drawing of the main buildings.

"I suggest we commence at the College.", Savannah stated after walking the map a couple of times. Dante jumped up on the table and rubbed his tail against

William's navy blue, velvet, frock coat, leaving strands of orange fur in the process.

"Dante seems to agree.", William surmised as he brushed the tail and fur away. William liked cats, just not the fur on his glorious clothes. "Actually, I was going to suggest the same thing. I know how excited you are about seeing the College and its professors."

"I do hope some of them are on campus today. I think it is about time I spoke with one about my curricula. Naturally, they will advise me as to which is the best course of study. I should like to get right into a series of philosophy classes. I have never been very good at math, though; I guess now is the best time of all to become better, do you agree?", she asked William as she climbed off the table.

She gathered her notepad, sketchbook, pens and drawing pencils and placed them into her bag. Just in case something seemed nice to sketch, she wanted to be ready. She also packed her hand mirror and an extra a shawl, in case it became chillier. So busy getting all of her things together, she hadn't noticed that William had made no comment as to her studies. Instead, he was looking at her very kindly. It seemed he had something sad to tell her.

"She is so happy.", he thought to himself. "I shall tell her later.", he told himself.

"Savannah dear, I will get my cloak and I shall meet you on the steps."

He said, "Good day!", to Mrs. Pritchen, who was gathering her baskets to take to market, patted Dante on the head and went above stairs to grab his cloak. Savannah also bid everyone a nice day.

"Dante, will you be back for dinner?", she asked on her way out the door.

"Of course I will. Tonight is seafood; I would not miss it for the world. I might see you around town. I have to visit a sick friend at the College. He is an affable mouse named Bartholomew and lives in a wonderful magnolia on the grounds. Maybe, if you have time, you can entreat us to a short visit. He would love to meet a new friend.", Dante said.

"What happened to him?", Savannah wondered aloud.

"He was almost eaten!" Savannah gasped at this news. Dante continued, "There is a nasty dog in town who has been here for a few weeks and terrorizing the neighborhood."

"So he does know about Petruchio.", Savannah mumbled to herself.

"He caught Bartholomew in a garden near the church and carried him in his mouth for quite some time. When he got to a comfortable spot on campus, he spit him out so he could begin eating him. Luckily, I was walking behind some trees when I saw the whole incident. I knew the squeals well; Bartholomew and I have been friends for a long time. I ran to the scene and climbed a tree just above the dog's head. Not a moment too soon, I leapt on the beast's back with my claws extended. He was so surprised that he forgot all about Bartholomew and he escaped. Now, I am caring for him."

"He is not injured too badly, is he?", Savannah hoped.

"Not too badly. He has to use crutches and received some cuts and scrapes. Plus, he is still a little afraid to be alone. So, I help when I can. Well, I must be off. Lots to do today."

"Just so you know, I think I know the dog.", Savannah offered.

Dante stopped and turned around, "You do?".

"Yes. If he is a big, ugly and drooling mastiff, his name is Petruchio and he belongs to a very mean plantation owner and Royal councilor named Sir Roland Grahame."

"Wow! You must tell me more tonight. We shall discuss this dog and his owner after dinner, okay?", Dante waved *adieu* with his tail. "I have to go right now, though. I am visiting my mother and, what with Petruchio and all, she will be worried if I am late."

Savannah continued out the door, happy that she had already been able to help a new friend. She thought about poor Bartholomew and decided the well-mannered thing to do would be to pay him a visit and take him a goody.

After sitting on the steps outside for a bit, she realized that even with talking to Dante, she still beat William to the front door. Looking around the town, she thought today she would keep her eyes open for possible trees she could call home. As she was daydreaming about her new dream tree, she heard William bid, "Thank you for the fabulous breakfast!" to Mrs. Pritchen. Savannah was excited to hear more about Mrs. Pritchen's family tonight at dinner. All she knew was that Mrs. Pritchen sailed here from Scotland in the 1640's with her family. They arrived in Massachusetts and eventually ended up in Virginia planting tobacco. Her parents had long since passed away and husband had died as well just a few years ago. She was now all alone and had chosen to sell her very small plantation and open a tavern for travelers. Generally, it would have been unacceptable for a single woman to allow strange men into her home; however, Mrs. Pritchen was well-known to be quite respectable, rather elderly and could never turn away a hungry or tired voyager. Besides, as a widower, she was lonely and truly enjoyed the company. Williamsburg was so small at this time that all walks of society and financial backgrounds took rooms in the same rental houses. So Savannah was not surprised when she learned that previous boarders that month had been a wig maker and another was the son of a wealthy Dutch banker.

"Well, *chere amie*, shall we?", William asked as he bent down and offered his blue velvet arm. He had selected a matching, navy blue, velvet cloak. Savannah picked up the bottom of her skirt and hopped upon his arm.

"What a lovely cloak, Col. Byrd. Is it French?", she asked, scrutinizing the quality of the fabric, rubbing it gingerly yet thoroughly between her paws.

"*Mais bien-sur*! Now, before we begin our tour of Williamsburg I think I need another cup of café. More cocoa for you?"

"*Mais bien-sur!*", she smiled.

The two friends turned left and headed down the road toward the College of William and Mary. The main road was not home to too many buildings, just a few private residences here, a merchant there, a blacksmith and a small number of other tradesmen's shops. Still, the street was busy and full with all walks of life: noblemen, children, men of the church, goodewives, slaves, merchants, and tradesmen. They were all on their way to do very different things on this lively, spring morning. William informed this road was called very simply, the Main Street.

On the way to the College, William and Savannah happened upon a seller of edibles and beverages. In talking to this purveyor, William and Savannah learned he was a free black named Anthony who had been released after decades of service to a tobacco planter. It seems Anthony had saved his master's life one evening when, while attending the dinner table, he saw Mr. Main choking on a pheasant bone.

"You wouldn't have believed it!", Anthony recalled with enthusiasm. (He loved telling this story.) "I don't really remember how I did it, but somehow I ran from the other end of the table, where I was fanning Mrs. Main, it was real hot that night, and I grabbed Master from the back." The storyteller entranced Savannah. "Then, I pushed the chair out of the way and told Master he'd be okay. I told him Anthony won't let nothing happen to him. I remember seeing a doctorman back in Carolina do this to another Master when I was a young boy.", Anthony assumed the position, acting out the situation. "I wrapped my arms around Master and just hit him with my fists in his stomach, like this.", he emphasized by hitting himself lightly in the stomach with clenched fists. "Eventually, a big ol' piece of pheasant come flying outta his mouth." Anthony always paused at this point to allow sufficient reaction.

"That is quite commendable character, Anthony. I too, would have set you free.", approved William.

"Thank you, sir. I believe everybody got a right to live, even masters.", Anthony blushed a little.

"So then what?", asked Savannah eagerly.

"So then, Master told me I can pack my belongings and go find anyplace to live I like, an I don't have to work no more. He even gave me papers that prove I'm a free man, just in case anyone thinks I'm lying, and a lot of people do." Anthony's tone changed to sadness. "Actually, I was a little sad at first. I knew I'd like to be free and not work sunup to sundown no more, but I also don't know

how to not work. I grew up a slave. Feeding myself an finding a roof gonna be hard. But then I think to myself that I have lots of skills, like making pies and cakes and hot drinks.", Anthony proudly displayed his stall and his spirits rose. "So, I hear Williamsburg's a growing town and think all these new people gonna to want pie and coffee. So here I am and making quite a nice living at that. Just bought myself a new coat and a pair of boots last month!".
Anthony held up a foot to show them one of the new boots.

Savannah and William found his story very inspirational, especially Savannah. She likened it to her new start in life. Of course, she had never been a slave and knew that Anthony's new start was much harder than her's. Still she felt close to Anthony and planned to support his business and buy goodies from him regularly. Remembering Bartholomew, she bought a small fruit tart, wrapped it up and tucked it in her bag.

William handed Anthony the pewter mug he always carried with him. Savannah dug into her bag and pulled out a small, sterling silver cup. She handed it to William whom handed it to Anthony. Very carefully, he poured a bit of hot water from the fire and into Savannah's cup. Then, he dropped a spoonful of cocoa powder, stirred it and handed it back to Savannah very gingerly.

"Thank you so very much, Anthony. It smells delicious, different yet delicious." Savannah breathed in the scent dramatically and smiled at another new friend, Anthony.

"You're very welcome, Miss Savannah. I keep a mint leaf in my jar of cocoa powder to give it a special taste. Col. Byrd, I have your coffee right here. I hope you find it acceptable. It comes all the way from west Africa." Anthony handed the pewter mug full of dark, strong coffee back to William. Just as Savannah had done, William smelled the coffee as though it was a bouquet of flowers and, very pleased, smiled and said, "Thank you, Anthony and good luck with your business. I will be sure to recommend you to my associates and acquaintances."

Anthony waved goodbye to the two friends as they walked away. They strolled down the street a bit further in silence, enjoying their drinks and people watching. As they neared the College, Savannah asked William to explain something to her.

"It is a very nice town, Col. Byrd, but what I do not understand is why it is so small. It just does not seem like an appropriate representative for the great crown of England. How will it grow?"

"That is an excellent observation. True, Williamsburg is small, provincial and not very regal. Remember though, it has not been the capital for more than a few years. It is not fair to compare it to the great capitals of Europe. The Romans established our dear London some seventeen-hundred years ago. Paris, although initially called Leutitia, was founded as a political center by the Gallo-Romans far back in the year 52AD. Even Amsterdam, though hundreds of years later and initially called Amstelledamme, was granted its charter in 1300AD, over four-hundred years ago.

Although this area has been peopled and utilized for centuries by Algonquin, Susquehanna, Catawba and many other tribes of Indians, it has never been set up in the European manner of a cultural, religious, academic, social and political center. You are accustomed to a very traditional, European-styled capital. Williamsburg, as run by Europeans, has only been a capital city for six years. Even if you include Jamestown in the chronology, we have been in existence for less than one hundred years. Still, it has already grown so much and will continue to do so. You shall see today that by the very physical nature of the College, Bruton Parish Church and the Capitol, Williamsburg can only continue to grow. Although there is not much to the town at the moment, the physical presence of these three buildings tells any visitor that this is an important, capital city anchored in the foundations of learning, religion and government. Many, many people will be coming to partake in our new government building. People will come to practice law, work in the courts and jails, and make the clothes they will wear. All these people will need to eat and drink and buy dry goods. By that very fact, more merchants will have to come to set up shops in town. Students will come to the College, they will need rooms to rent, taverns in which to dine. Professors will also need to eat, drink, shop and sleep. Business, government and education will bring new residents into the area and they will bring the money that will bring new business, and so on and so on.

"Just like you have moved here to participate in the capital and I have come here to experience a new life. You will probably buy writing supplies, leather goods, silver, shoes and things like that. I will have to buy all new furnishings, clothing, silver, shoe leather and the like. Is that what you mean?", Savannah recited dutifully.

"Exactly, my dear. Do not forget you shall also have to buy many other new items: books to pursue your studies, for one thing.", he reminded the scholarly squirrel.

Then, he got that look on his face again. She would be so disappointed when he told her. When should he tell her? He just didn't have the heart. He decided to put it off again. He thought maybe he could broach the subject of private tutors.

"Ooh, I had almost forgotten!", she squealed. " I have been so excited about, well, everything that I have yet to even begin thinking about what lessons I should take, and with whom."

"Of course, you know that I am happy to recommend some fine tutors to you. Latin, French,", William was politely interrupted by a slight throat clearing from Savannah. "Oh, that is right, I apologize, Mademoiselle. I know you are quite fluent in the language of the Sun King. However, there is always more to learn, in any discipline."

Savannah's ego was a little bruised, so she pouted for a moment. Then, being a very thinking squirrel, she realized how very correct William was and agreed to further her French studies.

"Perhaps I could study more French literature, you know, reading some very important works in the original French and not the translated English.", she offered diplomatically.

"Excellent thought.", concurred William. Happy to change the subject, he gestured toward the Main Street. With that, Miss Savannah Squirrel and Col. William Byrd II continued down the town's main road, prepared for a day full with new adventure and looking forward to learning many new things. Savannah kept a careful eye for Petruchio and that horrible Sir Grahame. She also kept an eye out for Dante. Hopefully, she would meet only Dante and not the slobbering beast today.

Chapter IV

Universities and colleges were Savannah's favorite type of institutions, next to museums. She loved reading, learning, studying and any form of work that would further her education and expand her worldview. Having done some research before she left London, Savannah learned that the College received a royal charter from King William and Queen Mary of England just previously in1693. There was one other school in America that was a bit older, but not by much. Harvard, she was told, was the name of that school and it was up in Massachusetts. Maybe Mrs. Pritchen knew about it; she'd have to ask her about it at dinner.

"Well, have you stretched your legs enough, Miss Savannah?", William asked her as she paced in front of the building, hands clasped behind her back, surveying the intricacies of its architecture. "If so, I think we should begin our tour.", William lowered his arm again, careful not to allow his great, ruffled sleeves drape in the dirt. Hunched down, they both looked around to see if anyone was close enough to notice a well-dressed squirrel running up a well-dressed gentleman's arm. Certain that the coast was clear, Savannah ran up his arm and nestled herself on his shoulder. They stood just outside the building and looked up at it. It was quite large, especially to a squirrel, and very beautiful. They walked across a small expanse of grass and came upon the entry steps to the building. There were six steps that led into a tall, brick, stately building. There were two huge front doors, beautiful and white. On each side of those great doors were twelve paned windows. The roof was hipped and had twelve dormer-windows. Savannah looked upward to a large structure on top of the building. Recalling some of her architecture lessons at home in London, she recognized the extension of the roof to be a cupola: a domelike structure that probably served as a belfry. She'd have to run up there and check it out when no one was looking. Sometimes there were lanterns in there to light the evening sky. Chances were good Dante could show her the way; if she wasn't too scared to venture out at night. Savannah didn't like being out of doors late at night.

"After you, Milady.", William's voice startled Savannah from her architectural and nocturnal ponderings.

He was holding open a great wooden door for her. Tearing her eyes away from the cupola, she bowed slightly to William and they entered through the double doors. Inside was an outside courtyard of sorts. Savannah saw a number of trees she thought might serve as potential homes. What better place to live than on college grounds? Knowledge and the spirit of great minds would surround her twenty-four hours a day!

"Come my dear, I would like to show you the Commons Room. First though, I think it best you hide in my pocket. There might be many men in there and we would not want them to find us strange."

Savannah jumped down his arm and into the huge pocket in the front of William's frock coat. It was gigantic, like a small bag all in itself. Actually, she was quite comfortable in there. She sat up just enough to see the surroundings. Her wig protruded just a bit, but was sufficiently covered by the big, floppy, lace cuffs of William's left cuff. He lifted a ruffle to see she was comfy and when she nodded she was ready, they walked into another building and above stairs to the Commons Room. From behind the intricate work of lace, Savannah saw quite a few very important looking men in fine clothing, all speaking very knowledgeably on one subject or another. They all wore simple, white, grey and, in some cases, yellowing wigs and carried books and leather portfolios full of papers with them. They also seemed to enjoy their own stories and conversations, for many of them would say something to another and then laugh and laugh as if they had just said something very witty. She didn't know who they were, but assumed they were indeed important. They seemed to assume to themselves they were important. As he passed, these talkative men would tip their tricorn hats to William. Once in a while, one would stop and tell William something presumably worthy and funny, laugh a great deal and then ask William about recent political events, or what the Queen had said recently about someone they knew. They all knew William and complimented him on his expensive attire. It was well known that William himself was important and close to the crown, so he was often consulted on matters of state.

She listened to a number of brief conversations and had very close views of various cuffs, ruffles and shoes. William's were the finest by far. Then, while studying a particularly gaudy ring on a particularly rotund finger, she heard a voice she recognized, and it was not a friendly one.

"Col. Byrd, my good man. What are you doing in this den of boredom?", a hearty laugh followed and then a hard slap on William's back.

This acquaintance had jovially slapped William on the back but had executed it so well that Savannah fell forward inside his pocket. Her wig shifted and covered half her face. Angrily, she fixed her wig and exhaled dramatically through pursed lips. Who could possibly be this rude? She had to see. She knew the voice, but still couldn't place it. Slowly, she pushed aside a piece of lace to see more clearly. Then, she smelled something awful. The smell was so bad she involuntarily fell back down into the pocket. Determined to discover the source of all this unpleasantness, she lifted herself once again, held her nose, lifted the lace and was greeted with a waft of warm, moist, smelly breath. Lifting the lace, she peered directly into the huge, brown, mucky eyes of Petruchio!

It was Rolly's voice she recognized! He was right there, talking to William while Petruchio stood there, waist level, dribbling and drooling all over the floor, narrowly missing Rolly's tacky shoes and looking right at Savannah. She was stunned into immobility. Petruchio hadn't reacted yet. He just stood there. How could he not know she was there, unless he was toying with her? She dared not move. Up above, Sir Rolly was going on and on about how useless the College was.

"Why on earth do we need more scholars? Silly, young men standing about discussing philosophy and life. Ha! What a ridiculous waste of time! Who cares what some old Greek had to say? Plato, Socrates, Aristotle: b-o-r-i-n-g, I tell you. The only thing young men need to understand is that where there is money there is power and where there is power there is money. Money, my good man, money is all that is necessary."

Sir Rolly laughed again and then pointed very loudly and rudely to one of the young professors in the room.

"Look at him! Are those rags he wears? He looks like a beggar! Who cares if he has read libraries full of old drivel and nonsense? What did all that education get him? He is a slob, an urchin in my estimation. It is an outrage we are even in the same room! I come to conduct very important royal business with a colleague who, for some awful reason chose to meet here, and I have to breathe the same air as that ragamuffin!", he sneered in the oblivious professor's direction.

"He shall sit over wine and tell us all boring stories about what this artist said to that philosopher for hours and hours. He obviously knows nothing of French or Italian fashion. It is truly disgusting that scholars are given any respect at all."

Savannah was fuming inside of William's pocket. She had never heard anyone so ignorant in all of her life. Sure, she liked nice clothing and pretty shoes, but she also knew her priorities and one of them was that there is nothing pretty about a hat if there is nothing going on inside the head it decorates. She thought it was a good time to jump out and inform Rolly that nobody liked him or his smelly dog, but Petruchio was still right there. Plus, she remembered her promise to help William's career and presenting herself to someone William might need in the future to help advance him in his quest for a possible governorship someday, she decided to bite her tongue and not say a word. This would be difficult though, for Sir Rolly just kept on and on. Savannah was having an emotional thunderstorm inside William's pocket; she was furious and disgusted with Sir Rolly for being so mind numbingly stupid about education, scared to death of Petruchio carrying her off in his mouth and disappointed in William for not asserting himself more.

William pushed Petruchio away one last time and in the process, nonchalantly looked in his pocket to check on Savannah. It was then he realized how poorly he was acting. Savannah's longing for knowledge and discovery of facts shone through her big brown eyes up at him. Of course education was important. He told Rolly so.

"With all due respect, Sir Grahame, you are wrong.", he plainly stated.

Sir Rolly stopped in the middle of fluffing his wig. Nobody had ever told him he was wrong before, at least no one below him on the social ladder.

"How dare you! What on earth are you saying?", he boomed.

William adjusted his waistcoat a bit and swallowed deeply.

"About scholars, everything you have said is wrong. I am a scholar, having been educated in the law in England and in finance in Holland. The finest men of England are scholars and the intellectual duelists and masters of the salons, not the merchants. Knowledge is the only thing that you can count on, not money."

William was feeling very proud of himself now. Savannah was thrilled over what she was hearing.

"Education and knowledge are for those with nothing else! Why you, of all people, Col. Byrd, should understand the importance of commerce. Your father's Indian trade has served you well. The very days you yourself brought as example, your days in Holland apprenticing in Dutch business law must prove to you the import of mercantilism.", he threw at him with a cocked smile. "What about your days at Perry and Lane in London?"

"If you recall, I grew frightfully bored with Dutch finance and my excursion into international trading with Perry and Lane left me even more bored. Discussion, debate, argument with your intellectual peers. Ah! That is the necessity of life!"

Rolly stammered various unintelligible utterances and shifted from foot to foot. He was beaten in his own argument and, having spent most of his days counting silver and not studying logic and debate, he could think of absolutely nothing particularly sharp to say.

All he could conjure was, "Money is the only thing you can count on!"

"I respectfully disagree, Sir Roland.", he emphasized the title of "Sir" in a very sarcastic manner. "Money can run out; knowledge and education will stay with even a poor man until his dying day."

Sir Rolly was outraged at this display of arrogance and disrespect. He had no retort to William's final argument. Instead, he manifested this inadequacy and anger in the only way he could think of: violence. He challenged William to a duel. William had not expected this reply, but knew what had to be done.

Gentlemen's etiquette allowed Sir Roland to demand a duel if he truly believed he was insulted.

Etiquette further dictated that William must accept, or be branded a cur, a coward. Considering his position in the community, William had to accept.

"Very well. If in truth you believe I have insulted you, your challenge is met.", William said with great dignity.

"Perhaps, if you reconsider your position and retract your statement, I will call off the duel.", Rolly offered with a long blink and false sincerity, a little nervous William actually accepted..

"I am truly, truly sorry, Sir Grahame.", William said.

Savannah couldn't believe her furry ears. How could he apologize to that lout?

William continued, "I am truly, truly sorry that you are so foolish and cannot see your own ignorance. I am also sorry that I cannot, in good conscience, retract my former statement. Send the pertinent details by way of your second and we shall duel. Swords, I assume ?"

Rolly didn't know what to say. In challenging William, he never dreamed he would accept.

"My second will call on you. Good day, Col. Byrd!", enunciating the title of "Col.", distinctly making clear the social gap betwixt the two .

He tapped his walking stick twice and whipped around so fast one of the feathers in his tricorn hit William lightly in the face. Wobbling out of the room, he tried to look dignified as his small, pointy, vertiginous shoes labored to carry him. His bright frock coat billowed as he strutted out the door. He looked like a great ship in full sail, setting course out of the harbor. On his way out, he pushed down a professor who was coming in the room.

"Out of my way, you sot!", he screeched as he stepped over the felled young man.

Petruchio followed involuntarily, looking over his shoulder at William's pocket and barking. Savannah decided to take a risk. She stuck her head out of the pocket, stuck her fingers in her ears, wiggled them and stuck her tongue out at Petruchio. Petruchio went crazy. He barked and barked until Sir Rolly yanked so hard on the leash it made Petruchio choke.

"Shut up , you stupid mutt!", they heard him say from down the hall.

Petruchio's barks and gags became fainter and fainter. The professor who had come in was so confused as William helped him up he just left without remembering why he came into the room in the first place. William saw no one else in the Common Room and told Savannah she could come out.

"You may come out.", he lifted her out and placed her on his shoulder. "Are you all right? Petruchio never touched you, did he?", he straightened her wig and patted her head.

"No, I am fine. Perhaps a bit smelly from his awful breath, but other than that I am fine. I cannot believe what you said to Rolly! I am so proud of you!", Savannah thought for moment and then her smile faded. "But now you have to duel. That is far too dangerous for such an argument with such a ridiculous man. I had a cousin who dueled another squirrel back in London and he, well, he died.", Savannah hugged William's arm. "You mustn't go, it is too dangerous!", she pleaded.

"I have no choice. The rules of etiquette state I must accept.", he explained.

"Who cares about the rules. Just do not go!", she continued to plead.

"The matter is not that simple, Savannah. In my position, there are certain guidelines and I crossed one by speaking to Sir Roland in that manner. I am proud of what I said and would not take it back, but the price I pay is to duel. It cannot be changed.", he said gallantly. "Do not worry, I am a very skilled swordsman. I have been studying with foils and rapiers since I was a wee lad at Felsted. I even fenced regularly with a group of my classmates while studying law at Middle Temple in London. This will not be a problem."

Obviously William was confident and seemed not to be concerned at all about the situation. Savannah could tell by his tone that the subject would be dropped. She would have to discuss this further with Dante tonight; maybe he would have an idea.

"I think we should go. There is still a great deal to see and I should like to sit in on a class a dear friend of mine is teaching before we go to Bruton Parish Church.

"A class? How exciting!", Savannah declared as she forgot about the problem at hand. "What kind of class?"

"It is a philosophy class, focusing on the teachings of Socrates.", he said as he motioned for her to jump back in the pocket.

"Just another old Greek, eh?", she mimicked Sir Rolly. They both laughed and walked out the door toward one of the below stairs classrooms.

Chapter V

Class was already in progress when they arrived at the door. William looked in his pocket and motioned for Savannah to be very quiet. Slowly, he walked into the classroom and took a seat in a small chair at the back of the room. The presiding professor looked up, recognized William and waved discreetly without breaking his discourse.

"So each of you will note that Plato had specific ideas about what is real and what is not. He believed that all we see around us is illusory and must be ignored so that we might focus on that which is truly real: the soul.", the professor continued his lesson. "Plato said that everyday must be a progression, to learn and evolve always. Everything is becoming something else, nothing is the same."

Savannah listened carefully to this from inside the pocket and wished so much she could jump out, take a seat and be a regular student starting right now. She saw that William's lace cuffs were overlaying the top of the pocket and thought that she could sneak a peek under ruffled cover. Looking over the top of the pocket and under the edge of the cuff, she saw the professor. He was very plain, dressed all in black, including black shoes and stockings and a black tricorn. He looked a little like a minister. His words were very powerful and he was obviously used to speaking in front of large groups of people. Searching the room while listening to the lecture, which, by the way, she found very exciting, she noticed something odd. There were some bench seats, similar to church pews and seated in them were about ten or twelve young men. Some were dressed very fancifully, obviously wealthy planters' or merchants' sons and some were dressed very simply; most likely, for these boys to be in school, it was a hardship on the rest of the family, studying rather than working and earning money for the family. The odd thing, though, was this: they were all young men. She saw not a single young woman. Now, Savannah knew that at Oxford and Cambridge no women were allowed, which was why she had private tutors. For some reason, most likely denial, she hadn't even considered that would be a rule here in America. America was supposed to be different. Perhaps it was just a coincidence; she would ask William about it as soon as it was safe. Still, she had a sick feeling in her tummy. What if she wasn't allowed to attend William and Mary? What would she do? Her dream was to begin a new life here in Virginia and part of that evolution was to receive a higher education. Slowly, she sank back into William's pocket.

Above, William felt very sad. He had been watching the joy in here face as she listened to the lecture and knew instantly what she was thinking when she scanned the room. He saw her smile melt and her cheeks droop and then saw her slide back into his pocket. He had been putting off telling her the rule barring women from the school for some time now. He just hadn't had the heart. It was time to be honest. After he talked to his friend Reverend Blair for a moment, he would walk Savannah to the Bruton Parish Church and he would try to explain the reasoning behind the rule.

"And so in closing, gentlemen, who remembers why we call an institution of higher learning an *academy*? Anyone, anyone?"

A young man with golden hair, tied loosely with a brown, silk bow and wearing a tasteful, brown, brocade frock coat raised his hand.

"Yes, Master Whitney, tell us why it is called an *academy*.", Reverend Blair demanded.

"Plato was fond of teaching and discussing philosophy with anyone who would listen and often he would have large groups of men come to his house for dinners where they would talk about what is real and what is justice and so on, for hours. Eventually, because his house was widely known as a space where grown-up men could come to learn, he came to be known as the first professor. Strangely enough, although I know not why, he called his house *Academy*. So, *academy* became synonymous with a place for young men to learn. The name has been with us ever since."

The young man sat down, pleased with himself for knowing the answer. The young gentlemen around him nodded at the answer, assuring the professor they too knew the answer, they just hadn't raised their hands quickly enough. From within the pocket, Savannah found this bit of knowledge very interesting, but sat with her arms folded and acted as though she already knew this and how very boring it all was.

"Excellent answer, Master Whitney. Well, with that, I bid you all a fine lunch and expect to see all of you in mathematics in one hour. Remember, gentlemen, when you return to this room for math class, be mindful of what Plato said about math."

All the students, gathering their books and bags, recited in a united drone, "Let no one enter here who is ignorant of mathematics."

The professor laughed aloud, proud of his indoctrination and walked toward William. Eagerly, he grabbed William's right hand and shook it vigorously with both hands.

"Col. Byrd, my good and dear friend! How long has it been? I thought we would have seen each other much sooner than this! How is Westover?"

"The land is excellent and the crops are said to be explosive this year.", William answered.

"As long as we can keep those wretched squirrels away from everything, eh?", the Reverend joked.

William winced as Savannah kicked him from inside the pocket. She was not having a very good introduction to the College. First Petruchio and Sir Rolly, the strange suspicion of 'no girls allowed' and now this 'wretched squirrel' business. Life was not going to be quite as simple as she had thought.

"It has been a good while, Reverend Blair.", William ignored the subtle, painful messages. "I see your work with the Virginia Assembly has paid off. The College looks wonderful."

"It took some negotiating, but when the Assembly sent me to London to persuade our good and gentle King William and Queen Mary to found an American college, our Royal Highnesses deigned it a good plan. As you know, I cannot be minister forever and the Church of Virginia must be furnished with a seminary of ministers of the gospel. What better place than our own College of William and Mary."

Savannah had now uncrossed her arms, crawled to the top of the pocket, careful not to be seen by the obvious squirrel non-friend, and listened intently. She had wondered exactly how the school came to be here.

"Indeed,", agreed William, "the Church of Virginia needs a respectable college to train future ministers. Besides, the youth of our colony must be well educated in good letters, manners and the Christian faith. Who else will teach all of this to the Western Indians?"

Savannah thought that seemed a little presumptuous. The Indians she had heard of were skilled artisans, many spoke French and had a religion already. Still, she could not reasonably argue with the Church and Crown of England and decided it best to keep quiet at this point. She might discuss this later, too, with William.

"So, Reverend, you have been teaching for how long, now?", William wondered as he looked around at the wooden floor, wooden benches and wooden podium.

"I have been with the College since the year of its charter: 1693. Although, as you know, classes have only commenced in these walls since 1700, just five years ago. But I have been part of the process since the charter in '93 through the construction which began in 1695 and now as a professor.", he said proudly.

"You seem to have a lot of classes to teach, besides your duties within the Church and local affairs; have you time for your home and self?", William seemed concerned for his old friend.

"True, I am teaching quite a bit, but we do have some other professors, including Prof. John Hodges and Mungo Inglis, over at the young boys' Grammar School. The young boys must do well there and be prepared in mathematics, geography, penmanship, Latin and Greek before they can come over here for law and philosophy classes.", he reminded William.

"Of course. They cannot learn about ancient Greece, Medieval Crusades or the great Italians like Galileo and daVinci if they know not where Greece, the Holy Land or Italy is.", he added.

"You would make a fine professor, Col. Byrd. We have need of a law professor should you become interested.", the Reverend offered.

"I shall keep that in mind. However, I have a great deal of work to do as Receiver-General. In fact, I should be off as we speak. Showing myself around town, you know.", he apologized.

"Understood, understood. I must ready myself for my mathematics class. We are beginning the theorems of Pythagoras today.", he said with a wicked laugh. "Let no one enter here who is ignorant of mathematics.", he recited, laughing still.

They made plans to have dinner at Mrs. Pritchen's one night, shook hands once again with the great emotion of old friendship and each exited the classroom: William and the stealthy Savannah to the left, toward the campus exit, Reverend James Blair to the right, toward another classroom.

When Savannah was certain the coast was clear, she ran up William's sleeve with a most determined look on her face.

"I want to partake in all these studies here at William and Mary. What would I earn at the end of all my studies, if I attended here?", she asked, emphasizing the word 'if'. William got the message.

"You would receive a Bachelor of Arts degree, known as a B.A.", he said.

"How long would that take? The Bachelor degree, I mean.", Savannah asked, obviously taking mental notes.

Prolonging the inevitable, William continued to answer her queries.

"Four years, as long as you do well on your final written thesis and support it well in an oral exam."

William sensed that Savannah was becoming more and more anxious. He asked her to come sit with him under a huge magnolia tree. He brushed some felled flowers off a stump. They were large as platters, white and still perfumed. He sat, very carefully, on the little stump, certain to not tear the fine material or catch any lace of his knicker-ruffles on a piece of bark. His knickers remained in tact as Savannah jumped from his shoulder to his bent knee. Her skirt flounced and rustled as she made herself nervously comfortable, anticipating that which she already knew, yet really didn't want to hear aloud. He gently took her little paw in his gloved hand and decided to tell her the bad news.

"Savannah dear, I really do not wish to relay this to you,", he said with a deep breath, "but the first and foremost qualification for entry to the College is to be a male.", he gently informed her, petting her tail.

Savannah seemed stunned for a moment, even though she had already suspected as much. She looked at William with burgeoning tears in her big, brown, squirrel eyes.

"Why is it like that? Why can I not learn like everyone else? I expect this from the older institutions, but not a school in America. Is not everything supposed to be new and different?" William could see she was very upset.

He tried to explain why rules were the way they were.

"It just is not done here in Virginia, Savannah. Women are not allowed to be students at William and Mary. It is expected that girls and young women will be trained and educated in the realms of the home: cooking, mending, decorating and childcare."

"That is all very necessary and noble, but why can we not learn all that and philosophy?"

William didn't know what to say. He thought maybe lunch would ease the situation.

"I feel a tad peckish. We shall have some lunch and then continue our tour. While we walk to Bruton Parish Church, we can talk more about your situation. Maybe we can figure out a plan whereby you can study the same curricula, though not actually enrolled, and earn a Bachelor degree 'under the table', so to say.", William watched Savannah's downcast eyes, her pouting mouth twitching as she tried not to like the very attractive idea. "I wish I could change the rules for you. You make a fine point. Women should be allowed to learn whatever they want. True, women are still needed to help in the home, but there is no reason a degree in law or mathematics could not be earned.", he conceded.

"Do you think there could be women lawyers?", she asked excitedly.

"Well, I think women would make fine lawyers. However,", he said into her ear, "there are many, many gentlemen in this town who would disagree with us. You would have generations of people to convince that women should be anything other than mothers and goodewives."

"Perhaps, but I will commence studying as soon as I can. Perhaps I will be a lawyer someday.", she chirped.

She was thinking about lunch when she saw an orange blur. Running across the lawn, wearing a very handsome orange and yellow frock coat and matching tricorn hat, was Dante. He was heading directly for a large magnolia.

"Col. Byrd, what were you thinking for lunch?", she asked distractedly as she watched Dante.

"I think some good bread, a few pieces of ham and an apple might be enough to keep us full until dinner tonight. There is a seller near Anthony with just what we need for tasty sandwiches."

"Would you mind if I explored around here for a bit while you get our lunch?", she wondered, still focused on Dante, careful not to lose sight of him.

"That would be fine, as long as you feel comfortable being alone. What about Petruchio? What if he comes around sniffing?", he worried.

"No problem.", Savannah replied with false courage.

She had completely forgotten about Petruchio and was actually scared to death of running into him. She thought of poor Bartholomew and wondered what it felt like to be stuck in Petruchio's steamy, smelly, mucky mouth all the way down the Main Street.

"I shall run up a tree. He cannot get me up there.", she tried to assure both William and herself.

"I suppose. Let us meet in front of the Church in twenty minutes. You are certain you will be fine alone?", William double-checked.

"Certain. I shall be even better if that merchant happens to have any tarts for dessert."

Savannah waved goodbye to William as he headed away from the school, toward the merchants' area of town, Market Square, far past the church. She knew it would take him more than twenty minutes to get down there, buy the food and backtrack to the Church. Calculating in her head, she estimated she had a good thirty minutes to visit with Dante and Bartholomew, then run quickly to meet William.

Chapter VI

She waited until William was out of sight and then picked up the hem of her skirts and ran to the tree up which she saw Dante climb. Standing at the root of the giant oak, she whispered loudly, "Dante, are you up there?"

She heard some rustling and hoped it was indeed Dante, for it was way too much of a ruckus to be another squirrel.

"Savannah, is that you?", Dante peered through the leaves down at the ground.

"Yes, it is. Dante, I have not a great deal of time, but I should love to come up and visit. Is Bartholomew up there? May I join you?", she asked so politely. (Her mother taught her never to arrive unannounced.)

"Please do. We are just reading a story together."

Savannah ascended the tree without effort and entered a lovely living area within the boughs of the tree. Inside, it was dark and cool, with just enough light coming through the leaves to make it pleasant. There was a nice breeze rustling through the thick canopy of leaves above Bartholomew's bed. The canopy kept him safe from rain and the prying eyes of hawks and owls. Savannah thought it strange that a mouse would live in a tree, considering all the birds that were naturally inclined to prey upon him. The look on her face must have given this away because Bartholomew responded to her wonder.

"Yes, it is an odd place for a mouse. However, I have always lived in the ground and behind houses, for my entire life. Being high up in a tree just seemed like a dream. Up here, I can see everything; I feel like I am flying."

"What about the birds?", asked Savannah.

"Well, cats are my natural enemy ,too.", Bartholomew motioned toward Dante. "Just like Dante has become my friend instead of my enemy, so have some of the birds in the area. Those who do not like my presence, well, Dante and the friendly birds help protect me. Life is an adventure up here, worth a risk or two. Besides, that dullard Petruchio cannot climb trees."

Dante and Bartholomew laughed merrily. Savannah liked what Bartholomew had to say about adventures and risks. That was exactly what she was doing, leaving a life of luxury back in London and setting up a new life here in Virginia. She loved this "Virginia spirit", she had decided to call it.

"Where are my manners?", Dante scolded himself. "Please, have a seat."

He motioned toward a worn, but still elegant wing chair, upholstered in obviously high quality damask. She thanked Dante and sat with her skirts all around her at the edge of the chair. Then, Dante took off his tricorn, bent deeply into a bow and presented the two new friends to each other.

"Mr. Bartholomew Mouse, I would like to present Miss Savannah Squirrel. Miss Savannah Squirrel, Mr. Bartholomew Mouse."

Savannah curtsied and Bartholomew, since he couldn't get out of bed, nodded reverently.

"It is so nice to meet you, Miss Savannah. Thank you for coming to visit me during my recovery. Everything that hurts already feels better just knowing I have a new friend.", Bartholomew told her.

"Oh please, it is very special for me, too. I am new here in Virginia, as Dante may have told you, and I have almost no friends, except you and Dante."

All three smiled nervously at each other as sometimes happens when new acquaintances are introduced.

"Oh, by the way, I have something for you, Bartholomew.", Savannah broke the tension suddenly remembering the fruit tart she bought earlier that morning. "I hope you like raspberry."

She handed it to Bartholomew who smiled broadly.

"That is so kind of you. We shall cut it and share some over tea."

They all smiled at each other quietly again.

"Now that we are finished with formalities, how is your tour of Williamsburg going with Col. Byrd?", inquired Dante, licking his front paw and cleaning away some dust from his forehead, all with a wiggle of his nose.

"It is quite interesting. I have already learned a great deal about the College and how it was chartered by King William and Queen Mary in 1693 after, on behalf of the Virginia General Assembly, Reverend James Blair went to England to ask for a school.", Savannah proclaimed.

Dante and Bartholomew looked at each other, both very impressed.

"Why did we need a school?", asked Dante.

Savannah thought this a ridiculous question, but remembered to not be snobby all the time. Instead, she tried to intellectualize the situation and teach Dante why a school was necessary.

"Well, besides the basic necessity of having a formal institute in which to pursue all forms of knowledge and to better ourselves as individuals, the colony has need to help provide the Church of Virginia with ministers. Students of all kinds are there, though. Some are studying to become lawyers and some study everything so that they can be teachers or professors themselves. A lot of the wealthy sons receive an education there so they can go back to their plantations and homes to tutor their younger siblings."

"Wow. You sure have learned a lot for one afternoon. What are you supposed to be doing right now?", Bartholomew wondered, hoping she could stay for a while.

"I am to meet Col. Byrd for lunch in about twenty-five minutes in front of Bruton Parish Church. We are going to tour it before dinner tonight."

Savannah then became very serious. She walked to Bartholomew's bedside. It was a lovely bed. Dante had been able to locate a dollhouse-sized, four-poster bed. Dante said he found it when a local family moved. The little girl who moved with the family had a dollhouse and left a few furniture pieces behind. Knowing a number of small creatures, Dante set them aside, just in case. Bartholomew's bed was covered in brown and gold linens and blankets. On a light branch next to the bed rested a mahogany highboy where Bartholomew kept his stores of cheese, nuts and clean shirts. Bartholomew was wearing a long muslin shirt with very full sleeves. Savannah was admiring the brave little mouse when she remembered what she wanted to ask him.

"Bartholomew?", she asked kindly as she approached his bedside.

"Yes, Miss Savannah?", he answered.

"If you do not mind that I ask, are you still hurting from Petruchio's brutality?", she asked most sincerely.

"Only a little. I am comfortable if I stay relatively still. My hind legs hurt most of all. But as long as I have good friends to visit me, my lovely home in this wonderful tree and hot acorn soup sometimes, I should be in perfect health again within the month.", he smiled optimistically, cringing a bit at a twinge in his right leg.

"Savannah,", Dante addressed her, "you seem somewhat concerned. Bartholomew is not your only worry, is he?" Savannah turned toward her chair. She took her seat and a deep breath and began to tell the story of Petruchio and the pocket and how Sir Rolly insulted education and the educated and how William told him he was wrong. With each new development, Dante and Bartholomew either clapped or hissed, depending on the point in the recounting. Then, she told them the big news: the duel.

"He did not accept, did he?", asked Bartholomew anxiously.

"Of course he did, did he not? I mean, he would have to. Protocol dictates he must accept any challenge put forth, as long as he actually said what Rolly said he said.", lectured Dante.

"Yes, he did accept and I am most nervous about it.", Savannah confided.

The three friends thought about this in silence for a couple of minutes. Then, Dante stood up from his elaborate side chair, straightened his waistcoat, checked his pocket watch, tapped his cat-sized walking stick on the branch where he stood and made a proclamation.

"We must make a plan!", he said with an emphatic strike of his walking stick.

Savannah and Bartholomew snapped out of their thoughts at Dante's words.

"Sure,", he continued, "the duel is rightfully acceptable by all rules of manners and etiquette, however, this does not make it right ethically. Two men should not die because of differences of opinion. Is that not the thinking behind coming to America in the first place. We are all of different ideas, different lives, and different dreams. Now, certainly, none of us likes Sir Rolly, but he does not deserve to die by the sword because he is unintelligent and arrogant about it. On the same note, Col. Byrd cannot die by the sword because he disagrees with Rolly. Most importantly, Col. Byrd must be saved from having to duel, without destroying his honor. He cannot know we had a part in stopping this ridiculous bout."

With that, Dante tapped his walking stick twice and sat down.

"What a wonderful idea!", squealed Savannah, wishing she'd thought of it first. "A plan to stop the duel really is the only way."

"I want to help! I know I cannot do much,", Bartholomew looked apologetic, motioning with open hands to the bed enshrouding him, "but there must be something to do from here."

"We have much to discuss; but, Savannah, you are late.", Dante advised as he looked at his pocket watch.

Savannah jumped out of her chair, looked at Dante's watch as he held it out for her to see and said a quick goodbye to both new friends. She shook Bartholomew's paw and said she'd be back to visit soon. She told Dante she'd see him back at Mrs. Pritchen's for dinner and they would further discuss "the plan". As she ran down the trunk, she heard them yell, "Bye-bye!". She'd have to hurry, William would be worried, what with Petruchio and all. As she ran off the grounds of the College, she thought what a nice tree in which Bartholomew lived. A tree on college grounds would be magnificent. She wondered if there was room in Bartholomew's tree, on a completely different level, of course. She wanted her own home, but liked the idea of being close to a friend. Besides, Bartholomew could probably use a nearby pal.

"Oh, how I want to study all the important disciplines and arts. Just because I was born a girl, does not mean I long to know Latin and chemistry any less than a boy.", she stated indignantly to herself as she ran.

Egged on by the thought that she was not welcome, she was pretty certain she would choose a tree on the College grounds and take up all the knowledge she could whether they liked it or not. She would listen to their philosophical debates and scientific arguments. She would take notes and find out which books they read and which books they disliked, and why. She would receive the most prestigious education in Virginia whether she had a degree at the end of it or not.

Running toward the Bruton Parish Church, she suddenly felt very inspired: school, a possible new home, two new friends, and "the plan". It was all very exciting as she saw William come into view. She couldn't wait until after dinner tonight. Dante was certain to have some great ideas.

Chapter VII

William and Savannah finished their lunches and sat in silence for a few minutes, enjoying the light breeze of the afternoon and allowing their food to digest. William had a Virginia ham and goat cheese sandwich, an apple and some ale in his pewter mug. Savannah had a butternut-spread sandwich with a chunk of goat cheese on the side, half and apple and some fresh goat milk in her silver cup. After drinking her milk, she cleaned out the cup with her linen napkin and tied it to a ribbon on her skirt. Even though they were just outside the Church's graveyard, Savannah thought this was a pleasant lunch and thought she could eat outside regularly.

The Church was a small, but long brick building of Jacobean design. The structure was simple, very simple: nothing like the abbeys and cathedrals of Europe. To Savannah, it looked more like a brick barn than a church. Savannah noticed that while the grounds were comely with magnolia and oak trees, effusing a heady scent over the entire area, the church itself, besides being humble, was notably shabby and in need of great repairs. The small graveyard was a little rundown, also.

William stood up, brushed some breadcrumbs off his coat and knickers and invited Savannah to begin the next stop on their Williamsburg, get-acquainted tour.

"Are you ready to continue our tour?", he asked, lowering his arm for her to ascend.

Hesitantly, she started up his sleeve and asked, "Are you sure we shan't see anyone in there? I would loathe to get you into trouble.", she asked, slightly concerned.

"Not at this time of day. It should be empty. You know the routine just in case.", he practiced opening and closing his big pocket a number of times.

"It's not exactly la Cathedrale de Notre Dame, is it?", Savannah chuckled.

"No, nor is it Westminster Abbey, but it does say something special, in its own, wee way.", he lightly admonished. The two explorers stopped in front of the structure and surveyed its simplicity.

"It is an English church, is it not?", she inquired, feeling bad about being so judgmental and snobby. She really needed to work on that.

"Yes, it is a part of the Anglican church of England, called Episcopalian. The protection and faith of this church covers a very large area of Virginia. People from over ten square miles come here to worship. Even more than that during Publick Times."

"What are Publick Times, Col. Byrd?", Savannah wondered as she glanced hesitantly at the graveyard.

"Publick Times are the times when the General Assembly meets to hear court trials and dispense judgments and sometimes punishments for those convicted of crimes. Specifically, the months of April, June, October and December are the Publick Times.", he explained as they walked toward the front door. "Later, I will explain better what happens during each of those months. With regards to the Church, all the people who come to town during the Publick Times need a place to worship."

He turned his face toward the shoulder on which Savannah was sitting, and spoke very softly, as though he was revealing something very secret.

"You do know that since 1624 Virginia law has declared it mandatory for every Virginian, especially members of important social and political positions, to attend church regularly and help pay for its upkeep with their taxes, do you not?", he confided.

Looking at the rundown building, she thought perhaps some people had not been paying their taxes very well. As if reading her mind, perhaps her wriggled up nose as she scrutinized the church, William relayed more secret details.

"I understand the church may soon be reconstructed and enlarged to accommodate the ever growing Williamsburg population.".

He turned his head back toward the church and spoke again in a normal volume, "Of course, this probably will not happen for a few years, but it is being discussed by the vestry and the General Assembly. The concept of growth cannot be ignored."

"It is a rather small church for a capital city. How long has it been here?", Savannah questioned.

She wanted to know everything there was to know about Williamsburg. Being a squirrel of great forethought, she understood the important age in which she was living. She was becoming the member of a new community, a capital community, in a new land, with a new government and new ideas. Someday, she would want to tell stories of how it all began. She looked at William and patiently awaited his lecture.

"From what I understand, there was one other structure here before this one. It may have stood in a different place, but it served the same purpose. An Anglican house of worship, the first church was most certainly a wooden building.", William began as they strolled the outline of the church. "Built in 1660, this area was still called Middle Plantation, just as it was a mere six years ago. In 1674, the towns of Middletown and Marston combined their parishes, or church communities, to form one parish and all came here to worship."

"Why the name Bruton? Was that somebody's name?", she asked as her eyes purveyed more trees. A tree on church grounds might be very nice, too.

"Indirectly, yes. The governor at that time, before our current Governor Nott, was Governor William Berkley. Virginia's secretary was Thomas Ludwell. Both of these important men were from a town in England called Bruton. So, the parish was named Bruton Parish.", William continued as he slowly walked the grounds, Savannah still on his shoulder. He tapped his walking stick on the street with perfect rhythm.

Tearing her eyes away from a very comfortable looking magnolia, Savannah looked at the church wall and found an inconsistency in William's teachings.

"You mentioned it was probably made of wood. This is definitely brick.", she deducted.

"I have yet to finish, my dear.", he chided her in good humor.

"Oh.", she said demurely.

"There was a very generous gentleman by the name of John Page.", he continued. " In the year of 1677, he donated a great deal of money and land to the parish. The church vestry ordered that a more stable brick church be built with John Page's money on his land. By November of 1683, it was built. January 1684 was when Reverend Rowland Jones dedicated the church officially open for worship. He was this structure's first rector."

Savannah ran down William's arm and walking stick. She wanted a closer look at the building.

"May we go inside? I would like to see the pews.", she requested, steps ahead of William and already walking toward the front doors.

"Of course. Just be careful of the graveyard."

He knew she had been eyeing it nervously. She whipped her head around so fast her powdered wig shifted slightly. Then, she saw William smiling.

"That's not funny!", she pouted and picked up her skirt so as not to drag its silk on the dirt. She walked very quickly through the graveyard and toward the church doors. On her way, she felt compelled to slow down, even though she wanted away from the tombstones. Without conscious thought, she stopped to read a rather large headstone.

She read it aloud as William watched her, "Elizabeth Page, late wife of John Page of Yorke and daughter of Capt. Francis Page. The eleventh day of November, Anno Domini 1702 in the twenty years of her age."

She paused, her head bowed reverently and envisioned for a moment who this young Elizabeth might have been.

"Did you know her?", she asked William sadly.

"No, I cannot say I did.", he answered plainly.

She jumped to another headstone and read aloud once more, "Capt. Thomas Thorpe of Bruton Parish in the Dominion of Virginia. Seventh day of October, Anno 1693, aged forty-eight."

Looking around at a small multitude of tombstones, some large and from obviously wealthy families, some small and most likely from families who could barely afford the inscriptions themselves, she thought to herself how death was the great equalizer. Here, it made no difference how well-read, well-heeled or well-born one was. Here, all were equal.

"Graveyards are very sobering places.", she said simply and walked into the small wooden doors of the church.

Now, she felt safe. Looking around, she could see what William meant by the need to grow. The pews were few and small. This could not hold very many families. The interior was even more rundown than the exterior; twenty-one years weren't that many, she thought. Now, Savannah thought to herself and did a few calculations in her head. "If the College began its construction in 1695 and the Capitol is only just about finished,", she turned three-hundred and sixty degrees, taking in all of the church, "then this must be the oldest building in all of Williamsburg.". William thought to himself for a moment

"Let me think for a moment.", William tapped his cheek with a leather-gloved finger. After some calculations himself, he answered.

"While Middle Plantation had been here for over sixty years before it was renamed Williamsburg, it had only been a small village of scattered houses and shops. The only institutional building though was Bruton Parish Church. So, it would seem that, yes, the church is indeed the oldest, *institutional* building in Williamsburg."

Savannah appeared satisfied with the answer and, after sufficient time examining the inside of the church, suggested they move on toward the Capitol.

As they exited the church, Savannah shivered walking through the graveyard. What hadn't occurred to her previously was what a very small graveyard it was, perhaps to match the stature of the church itself.

"Compared with some of the graveyards I have seen at home in England, there do not seem to be very many people buried in here."

Savannah examined the church's trees as she awaited William's explanation. Though she did like the idea of a home on church property, the presence of a graveyard, however petite, seemed a sure harbinger of sleepless nights. Besides, the appeal of living amongst all those scholars was very strong.

"Well, I do know that prior to 1700 two-hundred and sixty burials were performed by Bruton Parish ministers."

Looking at the earth, still bare of much grass this early in spring, Savannah wondered if all two hundred and sixty, plus whomever had passed on in the last five years, were laid beneath her silk slippers. Reading her expression, William answered it.

"However, I do not know how many of those souls were buried here."

She looked somewhat concerned, as if to say, "If not here, where?"

"Most people bury their own family members on their own property.", William tried to explain. "We all want our loved ones close, even in the afterlife. Of course, many church officials have argued that were more people buried on church property, the time spent in the often lengthy travel involved to visit a parishioner's home each time a service is necessary, could be better utilized to serve the parish and its people with more efficiency here in town. I imagine as the town grows and the parish grows and more people worship here, that will change. More people will be buried in the churchyard than on family land. The whole area is changing, Savannah, and we are plumb in the middle of its new era.", William declared excitedly, grasping the history of it all.

"Col. Byrd!", a high, posh voice yelled out.

Without even thinking about it, Savannah went to hide in William's pocket, but it was too late. The voice's owner was fast approaching and would have seen. Being slightly hidden by William's wig, she thought the best plan was to jump off William's shoulder and into the magnolia tree behind them. Peering through the giant, waxen leaves, Savannah saw a tall, thin, very well-dressed man approach.

He wore an Emerald green frock coat and a contrasting ecru waistcoat. Both were evidently of fine and expensive quality. Upon closer inspection when he approached William, she could see he wore a blouse of ecru, Westminster lace with a frilly stock that blew over his shoulder as he walked and he had matching ruffles under his giant, golden-accented cuffs. His wig was pure white and secured tightly with a broad, gold, silk bow. His shoes were black and as high as William's, but with gold, instead of silver buckles. From within his breast pocket, with white-gloved hand he procured a rolled piece of parchment tied with black ribbon.

"You are Col. William Byrd II of Westover, are you not?", the proper young man enunciated perfectly.

"I am. May I ask for whom you speak?", William's aristocratic qualities came through innately.

He knew for whom this man spoke and was not pleased.

"I speak for Sir Roland Grahame.", he too emphasized the 'Sir'. Even the nobility's servants were snitty. "Your presence is hereby formally requested at five-thirty on the morning of the thirteenth day of March, in the clearing just north of the College. As you understand, this is in regards to matters previously addressed betwixt yourself and Sir Grahame. The matter is to be settled with the weapon of your choice.", he raised his eyebrows as though he had just offered William some sort of grand prize.

"Rapiers.", William stated regally.

"Very good. Is all of the preceeding information clear, Col. Byrd?"

"Perfectly. Grant Sir Grahame a pleasant evening and I shall next see him at five-thirty on the morning of the thirteenth. Good day to you."

Sir Roland's second turned crisply on his high heel and walked with self-appointed superiority down the gravel road. William laughed to himself. With the servant's sword swinging at his side, his walking stick flopping about each time before it hit the ground and his high heels, prancing clumsily as one only can on a gravel road, he really looked rather silly.

"What does this mean?", asked Savannah fearfully.

"It means I now have been challenged officially to a duel by Sir Roland Grahame. We are to duel in two days' time at 5:30 a.m. in a clearing just up that way.", he pointed elegantly with an open hand to the vast Virginia countryside just northwest of the Church.

"Are you still going?", she asked quietly, knowing they had already talked this point into the ground.

"You know I must. I do not enjoy it, nor do I anticipate the event with any relish; but, it is the way of society and I have no choice.", he paused thoughtfully for a moment, then said, "Perhaps we should finish our tour for today. I have a bit of work of do and it would serve me well if I fenced a bit before dinner this evening."

"Oooh, may I watch? I love fencing. If I do say so myself, I have a pretty nice *parry-three-riposte*.", she asked, forgetting the nature of his impromptu rehearsal.

"Perhaps another time, Savannah. When I have more time to teach and less to focus on my own game."

She understood instantly and once again felt ashamed for being such a ninny. She couldn't bear the thought of anything happening to William and thought she might cry right there at the Church. She leapt into William's pocket, directly from the tree and pretended to look for something in the bottom of it. William understood. He patted his pocket gently and turned to exit the grounds. They cleared the graveyard and turned to their left, continuing the walk east toward Mrs. Pritchen's house in the rusty, late-afternoon sun.

Chapter VIII

The daylight was just beginning to fade slightly. While the sky was still bright enough, there was little sun to be seen and Savannah was now wishing she had worn a heavier cloak. William's walking stick kept perfect time as they walked down the Main Street toward the Capitol in silence. William had a great deal on his mind and Savannah did not want to interrupt his thoughts. Instead, she looked up at all the trees from within his pocket. So many beautiful trees she had never seen in any place other than Virginia. Not even Scotland had trees like this. Once she had seen the forests of Bavaria and they came very close in density, but not in scale. Here in Virginia, it seemed the forests spread endlessly like the sea itself. What an amazing place! As she looked up at the fluttering leaves in the March breezes, she fantasized about a home in a tree next to Mrs. Pritchen's house. She would always have Dante and Mrs. Pritchen close by and the wonderful smells from her kitchen would be a nice touch, too. Still, she thought about Bartholomew and how he could certainly use a friend close to him. There was a lot of thought going into choosing a home and Savannah took it all very seriously. She couldn't just pick one and set up house; it had to be prime. All factors must be considered.

William broke the silence and the chill in the air, "Perhaps Mrs. Pritchen has been baking a lovely game pie today. Mmm, that with a healthy pile of steamed clams, some hot clam and corn chowder and a piece of steamy spoon bread would hit the spot just perfectly.", William envisioned aloud.

This sounded like an awful lot of food to a very small squirrel.

"A morsel of spoon bread, some chowder and a clam or two sounds very good to me. Do you think we will have wine?", she asked hopefully.

"I am certain of it; though, not too much for you, dear.", he advised.

Savannah was in agreement. She had been brought up on wine, as were many children of her day, but knew only a little was best. Besides, she preferred a nice serving of sheep's milk with her bread. As she thought about the milk and bread, she realized the sound of William's walking stick had abated. They arrived back at the home of their temporary landlord. Savannah and William simultaneously caught the smell of fresh seafood and bread being prepared. They looked at each and smiled excitedly with a "Yum!" in their eyes. Silently, through their eyes, they agreed not to mention the duel anymore tonight. Tonight would be peaceful.

Savannah spent most of the afternoon's remainder up in her room reading and writing to her parents. She sat at a small writing desk on a teeny stool. It was well equipped with a brass inkwell and a small pewter cup for her quills. While writing her letter, she paused for a moment to think about the best adjective she could use for the upcoming sentence. It was then, during that pause she heard a faint scratching at the door. Putting down her quill, she walked quietly to the door and listened. She couldn't just open the door; as much as she disliked it, she was still a secret to many in town. She waited and heard nothing. What if it was Petruchio or that horrible Sir Rolly, come to rub William's nose in the duel? It scratched again. Savannah backed up slowly. Surely if it was Petruchio, he could have sniffed her scent by now. This was a common game they "played" on board the ship during the journey from London. She would hide, he would sniff her whereabouts. Holding her breath, she backed up again, making sure to miss the section of the floorboard that creaked loudly, even with a small squirrel on it. As she was walking backwards, the door pushed open slightly, making an ominous squeak as it did so. Savannah froze.

The door pushed open again and Savannah waited for her moment of doom. As she waited, though, she noticed something odd. Usually, Petruchio's malodorous breath announced his presence. She couldn't smell anything bad. Actually, all she could smell was Mrs. Pritchen's cooking wafting up the stairs. Even in the midst of potential trauma, the thought of spoon bread was heady. Shaking her head and focusing on the current danger, she turned her attention back to the door. So, if this wasn't Petruchio, then who was it? Mrs. Pritchen would have knocked loudly and called Savannah's name politely; William would have done the same. She quickly scurried behind William's bed and waited, no longer in fear, just curious.

The door pushed itself open a final time and Savannah saw an elaborate white plume attached to an even more elaborate fur-trimmed tricorn hat, a hat that only reached as high as just below the doorknob. Savannah breathed a sigh of relief when she saw that under the tricorn was a forehead of smoothly combed, orange and white fur. It was Dante. His eyes surveyed the room and saw Savannah step out from behind the bed. Tipping his hat dramatically, he greeted the fair squirrel.

"Good evening to you, Miss Savannah. I trust I am not interrupting anything too important.", he stated as he replaced his hat upon his head.

"It was important, a letter to my parents, but it can wait. You frightened me half to death. I thought you were Petruchio or Sir Rolly! Do you not know to knock on a lady's door and call her name? One does not just intrude!", she admonished Dante as she went to her wee desk to straighten her writing papers.

"I am truly sorry, I merely wished to not disturb anyone, should they be sleeping."

With the replacement of his hat on his head, he had forgiven himself for his affront and continued on to business.

"Mrs. Pritchen tells me it will be less than one hour before we dine. I thought perhaps we could take this time to discuss 'the plan'. Have you the time?", he inquired, cleaning his paw and then his plume with said paw.

"I think we should discuss things as soon as is appropriate.", she said excitedly, having completely forgotten her indignation. "Sir Rolly's second presented Col. Byrd with the official challenge today. They are to meet the morning after next in a clearing north of the College.", Savannah advised. Dante thought about this for a minute and then leapt upon William's large writing desk. He cleaned one of his back paws before he spoke.

"First and foremost, we must stop the duel. Yet, how?", he thought aloud as he continued to clean all his paws.

"Yes, stop the duel, yet how?", Savannah repeated.

They both continued to think in silence. Then, Dante's eyes grew wide as he remembered something that just might help.

"A ship sails for London the same morning. What time is the duel set?", he asked, getting down to serious business.

"Five-thirty in the morning.", she answered with hope. "Why? What time does the ship leave?"

"Five o'clock sharp out of Jamestown. If we could get Rolly to want to board that ship, he would have to leave for Jamestown immediately. Not to mention the added bonus of Petruchio being gone for good as well!", Dante explained with such confidence and superiority, one would think the task already accomplished.

He leaped from the desk to the bed, drawing his own sword in mock duel and shouting, "Ha-ha!".

"How splendid! We save Col. Byrd's honor, life and standing in the community whilst ridding everyone of Rolly

and Petruchio at the same time! "Tis magnificent!",
Savannah cried as she spun in circles, watching her skirts
expand and spin round and round. She stopped spinning as
she wondered aloud, "Except, how do we actually get him
on that ship?"

Dante halted his bed top fencing. He stood with one
leg cocked against the other and rested his sword tip on top
of a cocked boot at a dramatic angle. Looking to the air, his
chin high and proud, he resumed heavy thought once again.
Savannah hopped upon the bed next to where Dante stood
and thought hard, too. She tapped her finger on her chin,
certain that might help things along.

"We have to consider Sir Rolly.", Dante broke the
silence and leaped from the bed to a chair.

He sat with his legs crossed, showing off his
fabulous black boots. Resting one ruffled wrist upon the
chair back, he further explained.

"What does Rolly like?"

"Petruchio.", quipped Savannah.

"True,", he granted, "but what else. What would
make him leave here and go back to London?"

"It certainly is not nearly as posh or cultured here as
it is in London. Perhaps we could help point that out and
make him want to leave "the woods" as he calls Virginia."

"That is an excellent idea, yet he already knows this is no Londontown. Otherwise he would not refer to our fair home as "the woods" with such disdain. No, he is here because he has been requested to be so by the Queen herself. Rolly knows if he serves her well where asked, even in Virginia, he will receive great rewards in the end. He may be dimwitted, but he understands how to play his cards and wait for reward.", he expounded.

"I have heard Col. Byrd mention that those in service of the Queen and the Royal Governor may be rewarded with influential posts, grand plantations of tobacco and priceless quantities of land to build even their own towns if they wish.", Savannah added.

"This is true. Chances are good Rolly is awaiting something quite substantial if he is willing to rough it in the New World. We have got to think harder. What else does Rolly love? Besides money and power and Petruchio? This will take some thought.", Dante worried and cleaned his tail casually.

Just then, Mrs. Pritchen's friendly voice could be heard climbing the stairs.

"Dante, Savannah, Col. Byrd has arrived and we are ready to dine. Please make sure your paws are clean and join us at the table."

The smells of a fantastic seafood meal followed her directives.

"Be thinking on this over dinner, Dante. Let us meet after dessert and tea in the herb garden out back. We must come up with a plan that we can enact at once tomorrow morning. We have very little time and I am very worried.", she almost cried, but kept her composure.

Dante felt very bad for her and tried to assuage her fears.

"You must remember, that even if Rolly does not board that ship, which he will,", he added quickly, noting the terror in her big squirrel eyes, "Col. Byrd is one of the finest swordsmen in the colony, and abroad. He is younger than Rolly, more fit than Rolly and less arrogant, which means he will be more thoughtful and take his time. All in all, he is a better duelist than Rolly. Still,", he thought realistically, "Rolly is good and there is no sense in taking unnecessary chances merely to adhere to ridiculous codes of conduct."

Dante sheathed his sword with great flourish, straightened his frock coat, shot his ruffled cuffs and held open the door for Savannah while bowing with a deep and dramatic sweep of his hat. Just then, Savannah thought of a new meaning for the words "Virginia ham". With a hungry

tummy and a quick fluffing of her wig, she accepted
Dante's invitation down the stairs and off they went to join
Col. Byrd and Mrs. Pritchen for dinner.

Chapter IX

Mrs. Pritchen set a plain, yet lovely dinner table. Both
Savannah and William were accustomed to the finest of
table settings: exquisite English china, imported French
silver, exotic and odd pieces from the Orient. Still, Mrs.
Pritchen had beautifully simple items on her table.
Savannah liked the understated comfort of pewter. There
was a great deal of pewter on the table. Pewter plates,
porringers for the chowder, plates for the porringers, even
salt and pepper boxes of pewter. Their drinking vessels
were of pewter and saltglaze. They each had a blue-
patterned, saltglaze mug for milk and a pewter standing cup
for wine. Mrs. Pritchen had been using Bertram's fox-size
place settings for Savannah. The silverware was a touch
large for her paws, but she was able to work around that.
After all, foxes paws are a little larger than squirrels. In the
middle of the table was a tall muffineer. It looked like a
saltcellar, but was used mostly to sprinkle spices on food.
The fish would need a little extra spice probably, Mrs.
Pritchen advised.

Mrs. Pritchen served fish from a large trencher. It
smelled very good and full of butter. Next, came steamed
clams, raw oysters and a hot, steaming porringer of

chowder. This was Savannah's favorite and she ate as much as was ladylike. Her mother taught her to always leave a little bit in the bottom of the bowl. Right now, she wished she never learned that. The chowder was so good.

"Did you enjoy your day of exploring?", Mrs. Pritchen asked kindly as she served some steamy spoon bread from a yellow and brown, saltglaze bowl.

"Oh yes, thank you. We had a wonderful day!", Savannah answered, excited to relay her adventures. "We started with a cup of cocoa purchased from Anthony."

"I know Anthony well. I buy all of my coffee beans and tea from him.", she gestured toward a mahogany tea caddy on a nearby Queen Anne tea table. "I suggest his teas when you are ready to fill your own caddy. They are excellent; we shall have some tonight.", she added.

Savannah thanked her for the market advice and continued her tale.

"From there, we walked to the College where we sat in on a fabulous class about Plato, the Greek philosopher, taught by Col. Byrd's old friend, Reverend James Blair. I learned all about the 1693 royal charter that started the school. I also learned, later in the day, that I may not attend because I am not a boy.", she looked at William sadly.

"We have agreed that although we can not amend the rules of the College,", William broke in, "Savannah will follow a similar plan of study independently and essentially receive the same education. She is a very curious squirrel and loves to read. A higher education is only appropriate. It seems she had years and years of formal tutoring back in London in Latin, Greek, French, violin and mathematics. She is ready to move on to philosophy, ethics and law." William had grown very proud and fond of the little squirrel from London. All this talk of school reminded Savannah of a question she wanted to ask Mrs. Pritchen.

"I know you originally hail from the area known as Boston; do you know of a school called Harvard? I understand it is a little bit older than the College of William and Mary, but not by much. They say it is up in the colony of Massachusetts; is that the same thing as Boston?"

"Boston is indeed in the colony of Massachusetts, and I have seen Harvard College but only a few times. It is a stunning institution. America is well on its way to being grand competition for the schools of Europe."

She leaned into the table, as though getting ready to tell a secret.

"It is my belief that someday, years and years from now, even hundreds of years from today, that Harvard and the College of William and Mary will not only still be standing, but will be schools of great prestige and status. I predict many great men will attend these schools."

She sat back, nodded once as if her word was now in stone. She poured more wine around the table and continued with what she knew about Harvard.

"It has even been written to me that I have a young grandnephew that is attending there right now. He has in his dreams to be a great and powerful lawyer. The colony of Massachusetts is growing as are we and there is a constant need for young, professional men in society."

She relayed this proudly, as if she herself was attending Harvard. Savannah was happy for her grandnephew, but the fact stung her somewhat. She just didn't find the whole "no girls allowed" rule fair. Never mind that right now, she was enjoying her dinner and, as William said, she would educate herself in the exact manner of the College. Nothing said she couldn't sneak into as many lectures as possible.

"How are the oysters?", asked Mrs. Pritchen.

She was a proud cook and wanted everyone to be happy.

"They are of the perfect consistency and flavor, dear lady. Thank you for such a lovely dinner. Miss Savannah and I conducted a great deal of business today and spent great energy learning about this new capital city.", William graciously thanked her. "Tell Mrs. Pritchen what else you learned today, Savannah."

Always happy to share knowledge, she continued to relay her verbal tour. Dante seemed very impressed as he slowly stirred his soup with his spoon.

"Well, it seems the College was most likely inspired, or even designed by the English architect Sir Christopher Wren. It was built by the English contractor Thomas Hadley, but it is believed by those in the know, especially Reverend James Blair that Sir Wren inspired its design."

She thought for a minute, eyes fixed on the ceiling as she formulated a thought. Dante, William and Mrs. Pritchen waited patiently.

"I think the best part of the College tour was the class on Plato. Did you know that Plato believed mathematics to be very important, so important that he said, 'Let no one enter here who is ignorant of mathematics.'."

"Hoo!", reacted Mrs. Pritchen, "I wouldn't have been allowed into any of his classes. I am just awful in mathematics. I can add up my dry goods bills and that's about it. Hee-hee.", Mrs. Pritchen was not insecure or uncomfortable about her lack of knowledge in this area.

Savannah admired this trait. Mrs. Pritchen could make light of her intellectual shortcomings. Savannah would have to work on that. She was still young and silly sometimes and couldn't abide someone thinking she wasn't brilliant in *all* disciplines. Mrs. Pritchen continued to laugh and mimicked Plato's quote as she got up to bring more oysters from the cooking end of the common room.

"We also visited Bruton Parish Church.", Savannah yelled as Mrs. Pritchen left the room.

William gave Savannah a gently scolding look that reminded Savannah that ladies do not yell, ever, especially at the dinner table. Savannah looked downward and fumbled with her napkin. Dante snickered a bit at Savannah, all in good nature. Savannah's eyes looked up with her head still tilted down and stuck her tongue out at Dante. William saw this and shot Savannah another look, this one a little more serious. Savannah felt even worse now. Dante laughed aloud this time as he nonchalantly polished his knife with his napkin, rocking on his chair's back legs. Mrs. Pritchen broke the mood when she returned to the table with a plateful of oysters.

"Dante, please put all four legs of your chair on the ground.", Mrs. Pritchen scolded without even looking in Dante's direction.

This time Savannah giggled, under the watchful eye of William.

"Deary, I go to service there every Sunday morning. We'll all have to go together Sunday next.", Mrs. Pritchen insisted.

"I think that would be very nice, thank you. I would like to see it in full service.", Savannah accepted.

William thought to himself if he was going to keep her in line to be a proper young lady, that it was a pity she couldn't attend the College, as well. She would excel, whereas so many of those simpleminded, rude-mannered plantation owners' sons would just waste the experience. He could tell she would grow up to do great things and he knew it was his duty to help her all he could, in every respect socially and intellectually. He would start with a book. He would give her a copy of Plato's <u>Republic</u>. It was the perfect introduction to philosophy and law. She seemed to be intrigued by Plato and she would be well prepared for studies in those fields if she started with a complete understanding of his worldview.

Over dessert everyone talked of London, Massachusetts, government and oysters over tea and fruit tarts. Mrs. Pritchen served from an ebony-handled, silver teapot she had brought with her from Massachusetts. She said it was originally handcrafted in Boston and she'd had it for many years. The tarts were offered from a rimmed, silver compote and dished onto small, Delft-blue dessert plates. They were painted with the picture of a man fishing on a river near a castle. The tarts were yummy to Savannah. She loved fruit. The tea was a little bitter, but she was very gracious nonetheless and pretended it was the best tea she had ever sipped.

As they enjoyed their tea and tarts, Mrs. Pritchen told a story she had only recently heard of in a letter from Boston. It revolved around two young men and a horse race.

"From what my niece in Boston tells me, there was a horse race set between two wealthy, young men. Both their fathers were in the silver trade and both young men owned horses their fathers had purchased for them down here in Virginia. We do have some of the best horse country, you know.", she whispered aside to Savannah. "Well, it seems that over a little too much wine one night at a tavern, these two boys started bragging about their horses and fathers." Everyone sat in rapt attention, for Mrs. Pritchen was a very good storyteller.

"What did they wear?", asked Dante.

Mrs. Pritchen just laughed. She thought fashion was silly and non-utilitarian. That had no business in her story. Dante frowned and pictured riding habits in his head.

"Finally, someone in the tavern who was tired of listening to all this young, male bravado, suggested that they race each other and let that be the deciding factor. Well, everyone in the tavern thought it was a wonderful idea and the two gentlemen set a race for the next morning."

Still, the room was quiet.

"Then what, then what?", asked Savannah eagerly, sitting on the edge of her fauteuil.

"The next morning, the entire town turned out to watch the race around the Common. As they waited and waited, no one showed up. An hour went by before someone decided to go to their homes and find out what had happened."

"What had happened?", William found himself more interested than was proper.

"It turned out that both boys were 'sick' in bed. The truth was neither boy had ever really raced their horse, only pranced around town on it. Both were frightened the other would win the race and were afraid of looking foolish. Can you imagine such silliness in young men? It's that ridiculous pride that ruins many a man.", Mrs. Pritchen admonished the two strangers from Boston as she picked up empty tea cups and went to her washing bin. Simultaneously, Dante and Savannah looked at each other with knowing grins. They had their plan and couldn't wait to get out to the garden and discuss it.

The night ended with William reading a selection from one of his favorite books he carried with him always: "Henry V" by William Shakespeare. Savannah found it a bit heavy for late night reading, nonetheless it was Shakespeare and she enjoyed it immensely.

As soon as Mrs. Pritchen cleared all the dishes and William excused himself to drill some *parries*, *ripostes* and *point-practice* in his room, Dante and Savannah ran out to the backyard herb garden to share the unspoken but already finalized plan to rid the colony of Rolly and Petruchio, once and for all.

Chapter X

The garden smelled strong and pungent with the early smells of thyme, marjoram, fennel, lavender, rosemary and the many other herbs Mrs. Pritchen had planted in her herb garden. They were barely blooming, but the smells were wonderful. It was an early spring and the gardens were already looking lovely. Considering how much she cooked and baked, she had to have proper seasonings at the ready without having to go to market everyday. It was obvious by the sweet, almost humid air that spring was just waiting for its time. The potage, rose and herb gardens all buzzed with tiny flying bugs Savannah didn't recognize. She did recognize the gnats, mosquitoes and bees though and swatted at them with her great, fluffy tail. If she looked carefully enough, she caught glimpses of the most wonderful insects she had ever known: fireflies. She loved fireflies and could watch for them all night; yet, important business was at hand and Dante began first.

"I think we have our plan! Are you thinking that which I am thinking, Savannah?", he asked knowingly as he used his hat to whisk away a bumble bee.

"I believe so! What is the one thing Rolly loves more than money, power, expensive clothes and Petruchio?" They both answered at the same time.

"Himself!", they cheered.

Savannah continued their thoughts aloud.

"Rolly thinks himself the finest, most well-bred, well-dressed, enviable man about town. He could not stand the idea of losing at a duel against someone who was not a 'Sir'."

"Exactly,", Dante continued, "either way the duel turned out, he would be humiliated. If he was injured and William gave him quarters, called off the duel, he'd be ashamed to have received kindness in pity."

"If William did not call off the duel,", Savannah now took over, "and Rolly actually died, even in death he would writhe in humility that his was killed by Col. Byrd."

"His own vanity must be used against him. That is how we will send him home.", stated Dante with complete and utter confidence.

"Do you think he has thought of this already, though? I mean, losing to William. He is in obviously better shape.", Savannah had to look at all sides of an argument.

"I do not believe he has.", Dante pronounced. "Because he is so vain, the thought of losing to anyone other than Governor Nott would never even enter his mind. His vanity is our saving grace!"

Dante drew his sword from its sheath and fenced a mosquito that was hovering too close. Not convinced thoroughly, Savannah asked another question.

"If he has yet to even considered losing, how do we persuade him to consider it?", she pondered.

"Word of mouth, like that horse race in Boston. We must get so many people talking about Col. Byrd's excellence as a swordsman, that it will get back to Rolly directly; he will be so concerned he shall find a reason to sail back to London. We could use Bartholomew, my extended family in the area, Mrs. Pritchen, Anthony and anyone else we come across to spread the word. By tomorrow night, the whole town will be talking about William Byrd, the Gentleman Slayer!

"How can we get the adults to listen, though. I am not even supposed to be here. You know except for a few enlightened ones, most humans do not talk with animals. Mrs. Pritchen and Anthony could get the job done if we had more time. We have a mere day and a half, so it is vital to spread the rumor to as many humans as possible in the next thirty-six hours. What if Anthony and Mrs. Pritchen find the story too silly or boring to relay?", Savannah pondered aloud. "If she did think it interesting, she might ask William about his legendary past and he might figure out we are up to something. What can we do?"

Dante was sniffing some mint in another area of the garden. Savannah was looking at his back, waiting for him to turn around and answer when she noticed the plume in his hat turn toward the street. A sound had caught Dante's attention. Savannah heard only the normal sounds of daily life in a capital city. She thought it nothing out of the ordinary. Dante obviously thought it interesting because he stopped his sniffing, listened intently for a minute or two, then slowly turned around to address Savannah.

"Do you hear that?", he asked, eyebrows raised.

"What, the horses? The livestock? The blacksmith working? Sure, I hear it all the time. So?", she said with a touch of wonder.

"No, silly squirrel! The children! Children are the answer!"

Savannah just looked at Dante.

"Children, Savannah, children! They are the enlightened ones, they talk to us. Tell me, have you ever had trouble getting a little boy or girl to chat with you?"

"Why, no, I guess not.", she thought aloud.

"We can tell all the children of Williamsburg about the great William Byrd II, Gentleman Slayer!", he spoke as if it were a well-known ghost story. "In turn, they will chatter to their parents, tutors, governesses, churchmen, anyone who will listen. You know how they are, they love to tell stories."

"But the adults will think that is all it is, just a childish ghost-story."

Dante thought on that point. Then, he realized the added bonus of that fact.

"Even better! You know how children embellish. By the time they relay what has been told them, they will have turned it into the stuff of which medieval legends are made. Think about it. By sunrise after next, Col. Byrd II will have become notoriously feared as the nearly magical, Gentleman Slayer. It will be mere entertainment and party chatter to most folks; but, to Rolly, it will be all too horrible. Now, the thought of losing a duel will be thrust in his face. His ego and vanity will not allow him to chance death or, worse, humiliation.", Dante was very pleased with his vision of the whole scenario. Savannah finally agreed it was the best plan for the time involved.

"*C'est parfait*! We shall tell the children, the children will tell the adults and with any luck, Rolly will hear the rumor of the Gentleman Slayer before The Grand Anne sails back to London the morning after next.".

Savannah began to think about the logistics of their plan. "Who can we get to help us? There are quite a few children in town."

"Bartholomew, for one, can help. He can tell all the birds in his tree; they will fly away and tell the livestock and pets on the outskirts of town. The swine, bovines, equines, fowl and domestic animals will tell their farm children when they feed them in the morning. By breakfast, half the agricultural community will know about the Gentleman Slayer. When their parents and servants come to town tomorrow, they will begin gossiping as soon as they find another adult within earshot.", Dante devised.

"What about your family? Can they help?"

"Of course!", Dante slapped his forehead with one of his expensive gloves. "My family is huge! I have feline family all over this town. Betty, Regina, Victoria, Edward, Thomas, Gareth, Catrina and the others can spend all of tonight, as the adults sleep, telling our tale to all the neighborhood pets and livestock in town. When they wake in the morning, the children will hear the legend of the

Gentleman Slayer. By breakfast, the city adults will know the story as well as the country folks coming in to do business. By supper, the tale will be set in stone like that of King Arthur!"

"By the time the women are sitting down to quilt with each other and the men are in the taverns, the whole town will be buzzing. Most likely, from what Col. Byrd has told me, Rolly enjoys many an evening drinking claret. Col. Byrd also tells me there is a tavern here with fine claret and Rolly has plans to drink enough to test its quality. What better night than that before a duel. Surely he will brag about winning.", Savannah imagined.

"Too true! I forgot about his big mouth. He will do all the work for us. Someone is bound to tell him the legend as soon as he begins bragging.", Dante envisioned. "Of course, are not duels strictly *verboten*, you know, forbidden?", he whispered.

"I know they are not advertised. William has made it very clear that no one knows about this. That is why, I assume, the duel is to be fought so early in the morning in such a remote field."

"The more I think on the matter, Rolly is so full of himself, *verboten* or not, he shan't be able to resist telling a tavern full of gentlemen and a barmaid or two about his pending victory. Especially, if he is enjoying a bottle or two of wine.", Dante staggered, dramatizing the role of a drunken Sir Roland.

The two friends laughed until their sides ached. Then, Savannah heard the cry of an owl, which made her think of the birds in Bartholomew's tree.

"We should get going. If we can just get to Bartholomew and your family, the story will grow as we sleep. Let me grab my cloak and we shall begin the legend of,", Dante chimed in with his spookiest voice, " the Gentleman Slayer!"

Savannah ran inside, grabbed her blue velvet cloak, told Mrs. Pritchen she and Dante were going for a walk and scampered out the door. Dante was fencing fireflies when she returned.

"Halt!", she cried.

Like any proper fencer, Dante stopped fencing on the command.

"Are we ready?", Savannah asked.

"*En garde*, Monsieur Rolly!", he challenged the air in the *en garde* position.

He lunged and Savannah giggled. They entered the darkened street, lit only by a full moon and began the first step of 'the plan'.

That night, as William lay sleeping in his bed and Savannah in her miniature rice and tobacco bed that Mrs. Pritchen loaned her (one of Bertram's pieces), she thought about the network of storytelling taking place in and around Williamsburg. As she lay under her ivory, cotton coverlet, her tail, washed, brushed and smelling of lemon verbena, lay next to her on the pillow, she hoped with all her might that their plan would work. She looked up at her dear, dear friend and wanted him to be around for a very long time. Imagine, being challenged to a duel just for stating the obvious: knowledge is superior. The more she thought about it, of course Rolly didn't deserve to die in a duel just for being stupid. He needed to go back to London and leave Williamsburg alone.

Thinking about Williamsburg and its primitive state, she smiled and replayed the day of discovery in her head. Once she learned how the town would grow, she understood how important it would become. Everything had been so exciting in its odd, simple ways. There was so much to see and do in the coming days, as long as 'the plan' worked.

Looking around the room and at William sleeping soundly, she felt safe in Mrs. Pritchen's house. She loved her company, but she knew it was time to find a home of her own. Thinking about all the trees she had seen, she just couldn't make up her mind as to which one she would want to call home. Bartholomew's tree was very tempting as was any tree on the grounds of the College of William and Mary. The Church could be a peaceful home site. There was a particular magnolia tree so beautiful and fragrant that she could barely envision a more perfect home; nevertheless, except for Sunday mornings, it was pretty lonely there, and the graveyard was kind of creepy. One of those wonderful oaks on the Capitol grounds might prove to be a nice home, but it might be too busy there. True, she might have the opportunity to meet many influential people, once they realize squirrels are not bad; but, those endless woods that started outside the Capitol were even scarier than the graveyard. The College was in the lead: that one, great magnolia standing majestically at the entrance of Wren Building. The woods were far enough away not to scare her at night and the grounds wouldn't be as busy as the Capitol. Also, it wouldn't be as lonely as the Church. Bartholomew would be her neighbor and there would be plenty of people roaming hither and yon on a regular basis and they would all have very interesting things to say. It would be the best atmosphere for her studies. It was almost determined. Later, after the duel was taken care of, she would ask William's opinion. He would know what was best. Savannah, like Williamsburg itself, was looking forward to a wonderful new life, with wonderful new neighbors and a wonderful, unknown future. She closed her eyes, rested her head against her tail and fell to sleep, and in the night, dreamed that she was a dashing fencer, slaying ignorance across the Virginia countryside.

Dante was anxious to learn how the events of last night's communiqué fared. When it was still dark, before anyone else had awakened, he threw his black, velvet bavaroise on over his cotton, embroidered gown and left on his knitted nightcap. He ran out through the back gardens, nightcap extended in the wind, and went to his family's home in the basement of another tavern. Betty, Victoria and Edward were already awake. Everything had gone perfectly. The local pets were all scared of Petruchio and were willing to help in any way that would rid them of the slobbering beast for good.

Dante listened to the early morning air and heard the neighborhood dogs already barking the 'the plan' and the legend of the Gentleman Slayer to any animals who didn't get the message the night before. He thanked his family for all their hard work and made arrangements for everyone to meet that night at midnight in the Bruton Parish graveyard to discuss how the day turned out. He bowed and effortlessly ran the length of the Main Street to Bartholomew's tree.

The birds were already chattering as the first glimmers of morning light began streaking through the darkness. Bartholomew was awake, due to all the chirping. He told Dante the birds had thought 'the plan' a magnificent one and had only just returned from spreading the legend. Some had flown to Yorktown, others to Jamestown, and a few flew as a group up the banks of the James River, telling everything to the animals of the mighty James River plantations. The birds, and especially Bartholomew, were thrilled to be part of such a noble scheme. Certainly, they knew, as did anyone who knew Col. Byrd that he would be victorious in any challenge set before him. Still, no one liked Rolly or Petruchio and no one saw any reason to take unnecessary chances. William didn't have to know about their work, just be the unknowing benefactor of it.

Satisfied that the nocturnal execution of 'the plan' had gone according to schedule, he rushed back to house. Daylight was breaking at an increasing pace and he dared not be caught out of doors in his night garments. He made it back to the house and through the backyard gardens just as the first carriage rolled by the house. As he went above stairs to his room and looked out the window, he noticed the carriage was stopped at the front steps of Mrs. Pritchen's home. He heard movement below stairs and then heard the front door open and saw Mrs. Pritchen walk outside in the morning light to greet the traveler inside the coach.

"Savannah, are you awake?", William said in a loud whisper.

Savannah was wearing a stocking cap over her ears and was sleeping with a smile on her face.

"Savannah? We have more touring today. Time to wake up.", William nudged her tail slightly.

She stirred, rubbed her eyes and saw William walking to the door.

"*Bon matin, mon ami*!", she greeted him.

"*Bon matin a toi*, Mademoiselle. Are you ready for more learning today? I shall take you to the Capitol and show you our government's new functioning quarters.", he told her.

She sat up and immediately began to think about what to wear. The Capitol would certainly be full of very important people and she had to dress appropriately.

"By the way,", he added as he walked out the door, "Mrs. Pritchen has a new houseguest who has only joined us just this morning. I think you will enjoy his company. He is a member-elect of the House of Burgesses. Join us quickly, I smell a hearty broth cooking."

With that, he closed the door and left Savannah to dress for the day. Below stairs, Dante was waiting impatiently for Savannah to descend. He was most anxious to tell her the evening had gone very well. Besides, he wanted her to meet their new guest. The table was set for a simple breakfast of ham, eggs, dark bread and a thick soup made from last night's leftovers. The new houseguest was sitting opposite William and the two were talking as if they knew each other for ages. Considering their social stations and governmental positions, they had a great deal in common.

Mrs. Pritchen told the new guest all about Savannah and Dante before she agreed to rent him a room. As it happened, he himself had a traveling companion: a black Pomeranian named Ichabod. He and Dante already met in the kitchen and Dante thought him very proper and friendly. His attire was befitting the companion of an important Williamsburg politician. Ichabod wore a gold, voided velvet frock coat with matching waistcoat. Both were full-skirted and the coat sported large cuffs with gold buttons. He wore full, velvet breeches and carried a gold tricorn with a black plume under his arm. Dante discovered Ichabod was German and spent his formative years in Paris, which is where he met his traveling companion. They had toured all over Europe before moving to Virginia and being elected to the House of Burgesses. He and Ichabod were here to purchase a plantation on the James River. Staying at Mrs. Pritchen's would be a temporary arrangement until a proper home had been selected.

Savannah entered the common room just as Mrs. Pritchen was urging everyone to be seated. Savannah took her seat as Ichabod pulled out her chair. Dante thought that was very gentlemanly and wished he had done that first.

"Why thank you, sir. I do not believe we have been properly introduced.", Savannah said, looking at William.

"I am so sorry, Miss Savannah.", William replied.

William stood up and introduced the new guests to Savannah.

"Monsieur Edouard LeVau, I would like to present to you Miss Savannah Squirrel, previously of London, now resident of Williamsburg. Miss Savannah, Monsieur Edouard LeVau, formerly of Paris, now resident of

Williamsburg and member-elect of the House of
Burgesses."

The two bowed heads toward each other. Monsieur
LeVau stood halfway as he bowed.

"*Je suis enchatné, Mademoiselle.*", he expressed his
delight at her acquaintance.

"*Ah, excellent. C'est si gentil connaitre quelqu'un
avec qui je peux parler Francais.*", she said, thrilled there
was someone with whom she could speak French.

"I am sorry, I have forgotten my manners. I would
like to present to you my very good friend and traveling
companion, Monsieur Ichabod Wolfgang Crane DerVrie.",
Edouard gestured toward Ichabod, whom stood, bowed
over his place setting and took his seat again.

The table enjoyed wonderful conversation as the
new friends and colleagues ate and drank their fill for the
busy day ahead. Savannah and William had touring of the
Capitol, Mrs. Pritchen had more housekeeping, shopping
and cooking to tend to now that there were two more
guests. Edouard had introductions to make and business to
conduct at the Capitol and Ichabod accepted Dante's
invitation to introduce him to the town and some of its
quadruped inhabitants. As they were finishing their cocoa
and café, Edouard brought up a most apropos subject.

"So, Monsieur Byrd, I understand from my driver this morning that you are quite the swordsman. Is this true?"

Savannah dropped her cup on its saucer, making a loud clank. Dante choked on a sip of café before spitting some of it back into the cup. William finished his sip of café, dabbed the corners of his mouth and addressed Monsieur LeVau.

"A swordsman you say? I have been known to be somewhat deft with a blade. What a strange subject for your coachman to be on about so early in the day. Why the interest in my fencing abilities?", he asked with extreme curiosity.

"I know not. Once he learned we were staying at the same tavern as you, he told me his young daughter had told the family the legend of the Gentleman Slayer over the early breakfast he took before accommodating me.", Edouard explained.

"The Gentleman Slayer? Am I he?", William asked with a polite, almost condescending laugh.

"Indeed you are, sir. As I understand it, you have slain many an evil nobleman, and even a privateer or two with one deft *high parry-nine*. You offer elegant, quick, clean, and certain death by rapier.", Edouard recounted with spooky undertones, made all the spookier by his thick French accent.

"Well, did you hear that, Mrs. Pritchen? You have the Gentleman Slayer in your tavern. What do you think of that?", he asked jovially.

"Oooh, I'll be certain to keep your wine glass full lest you run me through for poor hostessing!"

Everybody laughed, Savannah and Dante very nervously, eyeing each other. It was obvious to Edouard, William was nothing of the sort and was as kind and gentle as could be.

"*Les enfants.*", Edouard shrugged his shoulders. "Children, they tell silly stories that adults are even sillier to believe. I suppose then I am safe to be in the same house as Le *Gentilhomme Meurtrier*?", again everyone laughed.

Still, William looked slightly disturbed. He wanted to know why such a story was being told about him. He had never slain a single person.

Everyone had left the table and each was departing for their various business of the day. Savannah and William were readying themselves to leave, but Dante still needed to tell Savannah about last night. What with all the introductions, French banter and Le *Gentilhomme Meurtrier,* he hadn't the chance . Obviously, the rumor mill worked very well. He pulled her quickly to the side as she was donning her cloak and following William out the door.

"Psst, Savannah.", Dante whispered as he tugged on her hood.

"What is it, Dante?", she pulled back her hood and placed it over her head.

"I wanted you to know, I talked to Bartholomew and my family this morning."

"Already?", she asked, looking at the great clock in the dining room. "When?"

"Very early, before light, in my nightgown even!", he erupted with a loud giggle that made William turn around.

"Are you coming, Miss Savannah?", William inquired.

"Yes, just presently." She turned back to Dante. "I must leave. What happened? How did it all go?"

"Extremely well! Some of the birds flew to Yorktown and Jamestown and the plantations, just to be thorough. You will hear dogs barking all day; they too are sending out the legend. Cross your fingers it all gets back to Rolly.", Dante nervously curled his tail around his sheathed sword.

"It has to work. Look at Edouard: in town only a few hours and he already knows the story.", Savannah reassured him.

"Do you think Col. Byrd suspected anything? He was certainly shocked by Mr. LeVau's recounting of the legend.", Dante worried. "He had an almost irritated look in his eyes, under his fine manners, of course.

"I noticed that look. I shall find out today as we tour. I suspect it is as we thought; he probably thinks Rolly has been bragging about the duel and someone has stood up to Rolly, telling people Col. Byrd is much better. Rumors come and go, *n'est ce pas*?"

Dante quickly told her about the rendezvous in the graveyard. Savannah ran after William and waved "Adieu" to Dante with crossed fingers. She was excited about the tour of the Capitol, but couldn't wait for the day to be over. Midnight in the graveyard, as scary as it sounded, was intriguing and she was most anxious to hear that 'the plan' kept going well through today.

Chapter XI

They stopped in front of what she assumed to be the Capitol, as this was the end of the road. Behind the structure stood more trees than she could count. For a moment, she thought how beautiful and peaceful and quiet a home in one of those trees would be. She would think about it as they strolled the grounds. She would also think about all the activity on the grounds. Even though "Publick Times" would not begin for another few weeks, the Capitol was full and busy with many a well-dressed gent, all chattering purposefully, seemingly enjoying their own opinions very much.

"Here it is, Miss Savannah. The seat of government for the Virginia colony. All that happens inside this building will be representative of our dear Queen Anne and her colonists in this new nation. It is as though we have merely brought part of England to America."

Although William was nobly proud of his English upbringing, he was also proud of his American connectivity. This was a constant source of conflict for William. He was American, but unmistakably British in character. He found attributes in both societies and in splitting his time between Europe and America, worked all amenities to his advantage. Here in Virginia, he was proud of the Capitol, meager as it was. He served as a member of the House of Burgesses back in 1696 before returning for a while to London. His father had been a member of the Council of State in Virginia and since his death just last year, William had returned to Virginia to inherit his estates and eventually would receive the appointment to take his father's place on the Council.

Even his great-great uncle, Thomas Stegg, Sr., was appointed to the King's Council in the middle years of the 17thCentury. As a young man of noble breeding, educated and trained in law and finances in London and Amsterdam, respectively, with a fine understanding of classical literature and as a distinguished, fashionable member of a burgeoning colony, a life of privileged, public service was quite apropos for Col. William Byrd II.

As Savannah and William walked the perimeter of the building, she watched the dapper men moving and talking busily around the outside of the Capitol. As they turned a corner toward the east side of the Capitol, there came into view a courtyard replete with far more gentlemen than at the Church or the College.

"This grassy avenue is called 'The Exchange'.",
William informed her. "It is a social area of sorts: a place
outside the Capitol, yet still on the grounds where men can
comfortably conduct financial and commercial business."

Notably, the gentlemen here were much more
fancifully dressed than the professors and masters at the
College. While the College men were dressed handsomely,
the lawyers, councilors, and legislators at the Capitol
looked more like William. They sported fine, expensive
looking frock coats of bright, lush colors. The cuffs of their
coats seemed almost absurd they were so huge, and the
ruffles that flowed from the cuffs were brilliant. Savannah
saw dizzyingly high shoes and jeweled buckles; the
walking sticks they all carried seemed very necessary
considering the heights of their shoes . Of course, as any
proper gentleman would have, they also all appeared to be
wearing swords. Savannah liked this atmosphere. It was so
powerful and important. Looking up at some of the trees,
she began to rethink the idea of a College tree. Imagine the
conversations she would hear on these grounds! The people
she would meet, the arguments and debates must be
astounding. After all, this is where legislature is debated
and consequently either fails or becomes law. This is where
prisoners stand trial and receive sentences or freedom. It

has even been heard that the pirates who prowl the nearby Chesapeake Bay and Carolina waters, should they be captured, will stand trial and punishment here. What an amazing home this could be. She would certainly give this option some serious thought.

"Savannah, I think it best if you assume the pocket-position. There are a number of my colleagues about this morning and until we all become better settled,. . .", Savannah interrupted him.

"I know, I know: 'Squirrels are not trusted by everyone.'", she recited monotonously. "I loathe tobacco! Why would I want to eat their crops?", she demanded, becoming more irritable with the concept of prejudice as she turned to run down his sleeve.

William gave her a sorrowful look and promised, with his eyes, that the hiding wouldn't last for long. Obligingly, she scampered down his coat, got tangled in the ecru, lace cuffs he had chosen for today and fell, head-first into the posh, velvet pocket. On her way into the pocket, she noticed William made a fine selection of attire for a day at the Capitol. His French-blue, velvet frock and breeches worked very nicely with the chocolate-brown, embroidered waistcoat he chose. The ecru lace was a nice change from the white lace he generally preferred and his hat sported a complimentary selection of ostrich plumes dyed the same blue and brown as his suit. Looking at her own chestnut-brown dress she had chosen, she thought they complimented each other nicely, not that anyone would see, she thought sourly to herself.

"Here comes someone I know, Savannah.", William alerted her. "Good morrow, Mr. Powell. Everything looks busy and in order this morning. Are you settled in town for the court sessions?"

"Just about, Col. Byrd.", he tipped his feathered tricorn simultaneously as did William. "I have taken a room at nearby MacIntosh's Tavern. It is small, but clean and suitable for my needs. You, good friend, where do you rest your boots?"

"I am staying with kind Mrs. Pritchen.", he answered.

"The name is familiar to me; I hear good things about her cooking.", Mr. Powell rubbed his considerable stomach.

"You are correct on that point. Her Virginia ham is delectable. Ask Monsieur LeVau; he has just joined us at Mrs. Pritchen's."

"Ah, the good Frenchman. I know Monsieur well as we dined many a night in Paris last year. Tell me, is he still talking without rest on the works of Rene Descartes?", he laughed.

"First thing this morning, as I was reading my Hebrew verses in the salon, he was reading his weathered binding of <u>Meditations</u>. He even asked me if I dreamed last night, and if so, was I certain I was now truly awake?"

Mr. Powell laughed, "Has he yet asked you if you are certain of your own knowledge, outside mathematics, that is? 'Truth in knowledge' is one of his favorite talking points."

"Not as of yet, but I shall keep my ears alerted.", William laughed kindly. Suddenly, a loud, authoritative and booming voice echoed across the courtyard at the two gentlemen, interrupting their discussion of French, rational philosophy.

"*En garde*, Monsieur! If it is not the Gentleman Slayer! Please, kind sir, I beg for quarters!"

A good-natured, well-fed, red-cheeked man of obvious prosperity and importance joined William and his old friend Mr. Powell. The newcomer slapped William hard on the back, jolting Savannah around in her pocket-seat.

"My stable lad tells me wild stories about the pirates and aristocrats you have cooled in the name of justice. Is this true, Gentleman Slayer?"

William was becoming very confused by all this talk. He was not a killer and couldn't figure out why these rumors had begun.

"Good Dr. Mitchell, I assure you I have neither slain nor cooled anyone in my days, much less a pirate."

Looking at his stopwatch, William feigned necessity to be elsewhere at that moment and made a most apologetic farewell.

"If you will both excuse me, gentlemen. I have an appointment with a young legislative aide who needs some aid himself. Until later, gentlemen."

They all bowed to each other and bid adieus. As William walked away, he could hear more talk of the Gentleman Slayer and hearty laughter following. While William was not generally offended by humor at his expense, this was different. He couldn't figure out how such a rumor could have gotten around town.

"Savannah, did you know I am a notorious pirate killer? Imagine that, me, a pirate killer!"

Saying it aloud sounded so silly it made him laugh and thought as long as it didn't affect his political or social standing, what could it hurt. He shrugged it off and walked the length of the Exchange, bowing and tipping his hat left and right. Savannah heard conversations ranging from the prices of café and tea to gossip from Queen Anne's court to whom's prized racehorse brought what amount at auction. Then, Savannah heard something very interesting. A gentleman with a very strong German accent asked William if it was true.

"Is what true?", William asked.

"I hear from my friends of the Governor that you will be dueling with Sir Roland Grahame. Is this so?", Herr Gerstl asked in hushed tones, his eyes darting back and forth amongst the crowd.

Now, it was common for gentlemen to duel, but it was not common to make it public knowledge, which is why Herr Gerstl spoke so quietly. William wondered how the German knew about the duel. William had made it a point not to mention it to anyone. Mrs. Pritchen did not know about it, Anthony did not know about it and the new houseguest, Monsieur LeVau hadn't mentioned it this morning, so he must not know. Savannah shifted nervously inside William's pocket. William stopped in his thoughts and looked down. Could Savannah have told someone? No, no one would have listened to a squirrel anyway.

He tapped his chin, leaned in close to Herr Gerstl and said, "Ghastly rumor, I can barely imagine how such talk came to be."

Herr Gerstl looked disappointed; a gory duel was always something to which one could look forward.

"Oh, well, there is much talk of this duel. Sir Roland has told many men in the tavern last night he will certainly win with all of his eyes behind his back."

Ah, Rolly. Now William knew. Rolly and his big mouth. What a donkey he was: living proof that money couldn't buy class. William talked his way out of this implication and left Herr Gerstl with wrinkled eyebrows and not too sure of what just happened.

William spent the next half-hour excusing himself from uncomfortable conversations and finally decided to admit, stealthily, he would be dueling Rolly, but it was a private affair in an undisclosed location. This seemed to bother many of the inquirers, as some felt they had been cheated out of the opportunity to witness excessive violence.

After William said "Good day" to a number of men, he walked well away from the Exchange and the building itself, so Savannah could crawl upon his shoulder without being noticed. He wished to point out some architectural features and the best way to view these was from a short distance. He chose to not speak of the duel or the alleged legend anymore. Instead, he focused on the Capitol's architecture.

"Come up to my shoulder. I would like to share something with you.", he requested.

She happily left the pocket and, moving some of his long, fluffy, black curls to the side, placed herself upon his blue velvet shoulder.

"Can you see the building well enough from where you sit?"

"Quite well. Have you finished your business within the Exchange? I am dying to see inside the Capitol.", she stated impatiently.

"I am finished with my social dealings. However, before we go inside, I would like to point out a few things. Do you notice the unique construction of the Capitol?", William asked, making a wide sweep toward the Capitol with his walking stick.

"Well, it does not look finished.", she answered honestly.

"True, true. If you look at the left side, the west wing, you will notice it is completed.", he pointed to his left. "Mr. Cary, the contractor, estimates it will be finished by autumn's harvest, but construction almost always exceeds allotted time constraints. Now, besides this fact, what else do you notice?"

"It is built in the Renaissance style. I can tell by the rounded arches and the tall cupola on top of the roof.", she stated proudly.

"Very true, except it is less embellished than traditional Renaissance. Remember, we are a young colony and without the resources of someplace like Venice or Paris. The architects have not built it with the telltale colonnades and fancy facades of more elaborate Renaissance buildings of Europe."

Savannah nodded, agreeing she had noticed it to be a little simple for the style.

"Actually, I had noticed that. I noticed something else, too. These two rounded chambers are very different. I have seen nothing like them before, except for the occasional chateau. Did the architects build them like that for a purpose, or just to look interesting?"

"It does serve a purpose. The outline of the Capitol was designed as a representation of the colony's new government."

Savannah blinked a couple of times. She was a very bright squirrel, but she didn't quite understand this. How could architecture have anything to do with politics?

"Shall we start at the beginning?", William noticed her confusion. "Let us stroll."

William's walking stick set the pace with a *click, click, click* as Savannah jumped back into his pocket and they walked toward the front door as he began to tell her the story of Virginia's government.

As they walked, they both heard a shrill and eerie laugh. Both bothered by its sound, they turned their heads toward the Exchange and saw its source. There stood Sir Roland Grahame, bedecked in a horribly bright shade of purple. As always, his towering shoes appeared too small and inadequate for his substantial frame. He stood there laughing heartily, Petruchio sitting in utter loyalty, as if he was waiting for his master to tell him the joke, certain it would be hilarious. Rolly continued to laugh and then, as William and Savannah decided to ignore him and walk on, abruptly stopped his laughter. This sudden silence made the two friends stop again in their tracks and look back at Sir Roland. To their wonder, Rolly and the tall, thin gentleman with whom he was talking, were looking directly at William. Savannah was sure she was far enough away that they wouldn't be able to see her perched on his shoulder.

The thin man was whispering something to Sir Roland that appeared, at least from a distance, to disturb him. Sir Roland quickly tugged on Petruchio's diamond leash and parted company with the thin man. Hastily, he exited the grounds of the Exchange, tottering on his shoes, which could barely keep up with his great calves. Sir Roland had no choice but to pass William on his way off the Capitol's grounds. Savannah pulled a ribbon-tied section of William's black curls and covered herself with them, obscuring her from unwanted viewing. As Sir Roland awkwardly teetered past William, papers falling from under his arm and not bothering to pick them up, he glared at William. Somewhere thought, behind that glare, William saw fear. Even Petruchio seemed to internalize Rolly's emotion. Instead of frothing and barking and pulling at his leash, he walked cowardly past William, as if he too was afraid. Rolly tripped down the street and dropped more papers, as William watched and thought to himself, "How very odd."

"Perhaps he has just learned I am the Gentleman Slayer.", William laughed and lifted his curls, releasing Savannah from their shroud of darkness. "Silliness, I tell you, pure silliness."

"Yes, silliness.", Savannah agreed nervously. "We should go inside, should we not?"

With that, they continued toward the Capitol's entrance.

Chapter XII

Walking slowly around the outside of the Capitol's entrance, and with thoughts of Rolly, the duel and the Gentleman Slayer subsided for the moment, William taught Savannah that Virginia's was the oldest representative government in America. Although the House of Burgesses had only met for the first time in Williamsburg just last year, before the Capitol was even ready to occupy, officially the House met for the very first time ever way back in 1619 when the capital of the Virginia colony was Jamestown. Savannah didn't know this and found it quite impressive. What she did know was that the fire, which burned the Jamestown Statehouse in 1698, was the main impetus that moved the capital city to Middle Plantation. That was about all she knew of the Capitol. She waited attentively to learn more.

"Notice the symmetry of the building, the way both sides look exactly the same, like a mirror image. Both sides are the same shape and size, both will have the same number of windows, both have hipped roofs and a dormer and they are balanced with a connecting walkway.", William pointed out fine details of the architecture.

Proud of her knowledge in the area of architecture, Savannah was a little embarrassed to ask about a term she didn't know.

"What exactly is a dormer?"

"A dormer is that small window with a roof on it, the one that looks like it is set within the roof.", William pointed upward.

"Ah, I see.", she said plainly. She should have known that and felt a bit silly for not knowing. "The cupola at the top of the connecting walkway, is just like the one on top of the College.", she reinstated her intelligence.

"You have an excellent eye for detail. Perhaps you will become an architect and design more buildings for Williamsburg." William tapped his walking stick and said, "Now, intelligent one, what does the plan of the building tell you about the plan of the government body it will hold?"

Savannah nodded slowly in contemplation and accepted the challenge of a pop quiz. Tapping her furry cheek with a glove, she pondered the question very seriously. Then, she hopped off William's shoulder and ran around all sides of the brick structure. This took a few minutes and William took the opportunity to chat with a fellow representative whom approached. Upon Savannah's return from exploration, William tipped his hat in farewell to his associate and turned to Savannah.

"Well, have you come to a conclusion? Remember, think about the symmetry, the equality of the elements.", he reminded her.

"I believe I have the answer.", she stated confidently. "The building is very balanced. One side is exactly the same as the other. In between the two is a strong and sturdy connection, a bridge, if you will."

William listened intently, as if he didn't already know the answer.

"The main thing to remember, like you said, is the symmetry, equality. That is the key: equality.", this word she said slowly and profoundly. "The two houses of government will be equal. Nothing can happen without consequence and no house shall act without affecting, or being affected by, the other. The bridge, I think, represents an area of ideology where the two houses come together."

Savannah curtsied slightly with a bit of arrogance, proud that she had answered well. William returned the gesture with a tip of his hat.

"You are a very insightful squirrel. That is correct. It is important that the government work together and help to grow a fair and balanced community, in the name of Queen Anne."

William smiled at Savannah. He admired her intelligence and attitude toward learning.

"Wait until we go inside, you will better understand what balance and equity truly mean in government."

William imparted more information to her as they continued the tour.

"You may need to know, in case you are in the building after nightfall, candles and fireplaces, even tobacco pipes to the resentment of many a legislator, have been outlawed within the Capitol building because of the fire danger. This is our only seat of government and it holds all the paperwork and records pertaining to just about every person and event in the colony. The Jamestown Statehouse burned down three times. This cannot happen again. Fire prevention is our best plan."

"How will any business be conducted, unless the full moon shines in just right? What about the damps? Those papers and documents and deeds will become mildewed and rotted with out the arid warmth of fire!", Savannah was visibly disturbed by this newly learned fact.

"They might, but mold is much easier to deal with than fire and smoke damage. We learned well from the past and this is what must now happen.", he stated with matter of fact.

They entered through the farthest left arch of the three that framed the bottom floor of the "bridge". They entered the first-floor chambers on the left. It was a stately and quietly powerful courtroom. It wasn't as opulent or large as some of the courtrooms she'd seen in London, but she could tell it was an immensely important room. The first thing Savannah noticed was three large, round, paned windows. She noticed these on the outside, but they seemed much larger from the inside. The walls were all paneled in lush, dark wood and were topped with magnificent moldings at the ceiling. At the very back of the room, just under the three round windows, was a semicircular bench that sat very high. Behind it were a number of majestic chairs. Savannah counted twelve. In front of that were two low benches for a jury and a table where, she assumed, the lawyers sat with their clients. The rest of the room was filled with benches so that the public could watch the trials. After all, this was a balanced government now and the months in which court was held were called 'Publick Times'. William informed Savannah this room was called the General Court and it was the highest court in the colony. William reminded her his father and great-great uncle both served as councilors. In here, the Council of the Royal Governor met twice a year, every April and October, to hear cases about criminal and civil conflicts. William told her the only way to get into one of those majestic, tall chairs was to have been appointed by King William III or, since 1702, by Queen Anne. Plus, once you were appointed, it was for life.

William suggested they head above stairs to the Council's Chamber. Savannah did wish they could spend more time in each room, but she was excited to see it all today and William told her she could sit in on any trial she liked, as long as she was quiet. April would be here next month and she would get to watch many, many trials. Thus, with only a touch of hesitation, she scurried up the staircase ahead of William. When she reached the top floor she found another remarkable room. This one however, was more posh and luxurious than the courtroom.

She was admiring the magnificent portraits and the huge gold chandelier when William strode up behind her and announced, "This is the Council Chamber. This is where the twelve, life-appointed colonists will convene to discuss legislature, or lawmaking. They also act as council of state to Governor Nott, assisting him on matters of the colony."

He walked to a table that stood in the middle of the floor. It was of oval shape and very large. Around its perimeter stood imposingly twelve high-backed, identical chairs, like small thrones. The backs were beautifully carved on top, while the remainder was cane-woven. Each chair had green velvet seats. On the table lay a thick, tapestry tablecloth. On top of this lay sterling silver inkwells, each with their own quill for writing and signing very important documents.

"Do you think I could come in here once in a while?", Savannah asked very politely, wringing her handkerchief in her hand nervously.

"That might be difficult to arrange. If you did observe, you would need to be extremely quiet and completely invisible. High-level meetings are to be held in here and the other councilors might not like the idea of prying eyes. Not to mention a number of these men own tobacco plantations and seeing a squirrel would not set well with them."

Savannah knew this before she even asked. The courtroom was set up for the public to watch. Not this room, though.

Then, he winked and said, "I shall see what I can do for the occasional visit.", emphasizing the word *occasional*.

Inside the Capitol was not too busy, but William suggested she hop into his pocket, for he heard voices becoming stronger and louder as they readied to enter another portion of the building. She gathered her skirt and flounces and dropped into a rather giant pocket of William's frock coat. It was quite comfortable and she even found half a peanut she hadn't noticed before.

She heard William's walking stick resonate as it struck the hardwood floor as they walked into another large room. She poked her head out of his pocket and saw another stunning room. Again, the focus of this room was a mighty table. This one was not nearly as luxurious as the Council Chamber. Because the room was not completely finished, its decor was minimal. The table had a mere green wool tablecloth and the chairs were much shorter and not nearly as decorative. Still, they were noble. Silver inkwells and quills sat in front of each chair here also.

"Will any of your friends spend time in here?", Savannah looked upward and asked, hoping for more viewing privileges.

"From time to time, yes. This room is the Conference Room. I do not know if you can tell from where you sit, but this is the second floor of the "bridge" that connects the West Wing, where we have just been, to the

East Wing, where we are going.", he explained, pointing from west to east.

"So this is what you meant by the architectural significance of the connecting 'bridge'. This room connects both wings of the Capitol!", she exclaimed, very pleased with herself for finally understanding.

"Exactly. We talked about how the construction of the Capitol was representative of the government. While this room connects the two wings of the building, it also connects the two wings of the government: the Council Chamber and the House of Burgesses. Together, they are called the General Assembly and in this room legislators come together to meet, pray and resolve any arguments or disagreement they have in legislature. Does that make sense?", he asked the top of her wig as she looked about the room.

"Perfect sense. It helps so much to actually come inside. I could explain it from outside, but not truly understand what I explained. Now I get it. Balance of structure equals balance of government."

She asked if they could see the House of Burgesses next. They left the "bridge" and peeked around the corner into a couple of committee rooms.

William said this was where the members would meet to discuss specific issues. The room was filled with some of the same gentlemen they met outside in the Exchange. They were all speaking on similar matters as they were outside: tobacco, cargo arriving from London, cargo and people sailing back to London on the Grand Anne tomorrow. Savannah wished someone would say Rolly was going to be on that ship.

Listening carefully to some of the conversations, Savannah learned that many a trial would soon be coming into town, even that of a pirate who was being held in the Public Gaol. When it seemed safe, she asked William about this.

Throwing her whispers as far as they could fly out of the pocket, she asked, "Is a pirate really going to be here?"

Pretending to search for something in his large pocket, he answered, "Yes, a couple of them. Plus a horse thief, many a debtor, Indians accused of murder and runaway slaves, not to mention a host of other men and women who are awaiting trial. If you would like to see the gaol, we may visit there when we have finished here."

Savannah instantly thought how fascinating it would be to see a real pirate, as long as William was always nearby. Weighing the options of knowledge over fear, she decided it would serve her best to visit the gaol and educate herself a bit more in the judiciary system of this new colony.

William promised Savannah they could visit the Public Gaol later in the day, but currently, it was becoming crowded inside the meeting room and he wanted to show her the House of Burgesses. Engaging in numerous demi-conversations, William bowed, tipped his hat and excused himself all the way across the wooden floor, his heels in an up-tempo, announcing his urgency to depart the room.

They descended the staircase and stepped into a room that was structurally identical to the General Court. Except, it was clearly still in the earlier stages of construction. The same three, round windows were there, but instead of a high bench, there was a space for a single, very tall chair. The perimeter of the room was lined with long benches of dark wood. It was very business-like even in its premature state. Even so, some clusters of gentleman stood conducting verbal business. Savannah felt bold enough to prop herself upon her arms and hang over the pocket, still shrouded by his massive ruffles. Tugging on those ruffles, she had a thousand questions floating in her head.

"How about this room? Who will meet in here regularly? This room seems a lot bigger. It is very cold in here. When are they going to finish building this room?", Savannah wondered, still riding in his pocket.

"This is the House of Burgesses. While the Queen appoints members of the Council to the Royal Governor, Virginia landowning gentlemen elect members of the House. Two men are elected from each county in Virginia, plus one man each from Jamestown, Williamsburg, Norfolk and the College. So, there will be quite a few more men in here than in the Council upstairs. Yes, it is cold and that east wall should be completed by summer."

"By then we shan't need a wall. If they discuss colonial legislature and the Governor's business upstairs, what do they discuss down here?"

This was becoming a little confusing to Savannah and she was not afraid to admit it.

"Are they not all the same people?"

"Somewhat. All represent the Queen but specifically, the Council represents the Royal Governor and the House of Burgesses represents the citizens of Virginia. Burgess is just another word for "citizen": the House of Citizens. Together, they make laws and decide upon events that will best serve the whole colony, under the distant eye of the British crown, *bien-sur*. For the most part though, we rule ourselves through these gentlemen in the Capitol."

Savannah digested all that information and then looked at the whole room again. It was sinking in and her political science lesson was becoming clearer.

"What about the space up front? Who will sit up there? The Royal Governor?", she pointed to a space which would presumably serve as a dominant seat of power. It was under the middle, round, paned window that was exactly the same as the window in the Courtroom.

"No. The Speaker of the House of Burgesses sits there. First, the members of the House of Burgesses go above stairs to take their oaths of office in the Council Chamber in the presence of the Councilors. Then, they come back below stairs and elect the Speaker amongst themselves. After the Royal Governor formally approves of their elected man, the Speaker takes his seat and the House of Burgesses may begin their work.

Savannah listened to all of this very intently and after a few moments declared simply, "I see."

Actually, it was all still pretty confusing. As she understood it all, everyone whom served at the Capitol did mostly the same thing, but in different rooms for different people. She knew it was more complex than that, but thus far, that was what she had determined. She couldn't understand exactly what they did and precisely for whom very clearly yet. William motioned for her to get down, someone was approaching them.

"Col. Byrd, how wonderful it is to see you!", a tall, red-haired gentleman said quietly. "I thought to myself on my journey down from home how I love this time of year, getting to see old friends and make new acquaintances in government. Indeed, I thought specifically of you, dear friend. How have you been?"

William was obviously pleased to see this man, an old friend from Virginia. His name was Mr. Curtis Gilbert, gentleman farmer from across the water. He hailed from an area called Accomack County on Virginia's Eastern Shore. Separated by the great Chesapeake Bay, Mr. Gilbert had to travel by ship from Accomack to Williamsburg. He spoke softly and elegantly and tended to shuffle his glances from his own dusty, brown shoes to William's blue-black wig, always a little too nervous to make direct eye contact. Savannah surmised he got on better with books than people.

"Dear Mr. Gilbert! It is a great joy to see a familiar face from across the Chesapeake. You look well. Mrs. Gilbert is not feeding you enough of your own Virginia

ham, however. Thin around the belt you always were.",
William jested with his friend, lightly patting the flat front
of Curtis' waistcoat.

"Mrs. Gilbert has prepared for me only the grandest
pies of game and meat and amazing portions of potatoes
and spoon bread. 'Tis the dancing, my friend. Four hours
dancing merrily with my daughters and wife whip even the
largest of men into shape.", Curtis' eyes dreamed visibly of
his wife and family.

William always liked Curtis Gilbert. It was easy to
see why he was elected by his peers to be a member of the
House of Burgesses. He was a cultured man of refinement
and ever loyal to those around him. It was said, even by and
of his political adversaries, that a harsh word was never
uttered.

"Speaking of fine meals, I would enjoy your
company at dinner this evening. Where are you staying this
time?", William invited, knowing Mrs. Pritchen expected
different diners from night to night during Publick Times.

"I am staying with relatives of Mrs. Gilbert. Yet, I
am certain they would be relieved to have one less mouth at
dinner this evening."

He bent close to William and whispered, as if the relatives were within earshot and he wished not to hurt their dignity.

"Their small cobbling shop is doing very poorly and all are in ration-mode until the outlook is better. There was a time just last year when they were making and selling an average of three pairs of shoes and boots day. Now, he can barely sell that in one week's time. With the colony's gentlemen coming into town in this next month, he looks forward to a surge in business. For now though, it is meager."

"It is indeed very kind of them to accommodate you under such circumstances. Do you help them with their creditors?", William inquired.

"I have tried, as you know I might, yet Jonathon, Mrs. Gilbert's young cousin, will not allow it. He is fiercely proud and would not have children see their father accepting charity, even from family.", Curtis shook his head. "Even when I insisted I would board at a tavern whilst in town, they insisted further and greater that I would stay with them. In truth, I am rather uncomfortable, for they will not charge me; whereas if another boarder were in my bed, they could expect countable shillings from him.

William did not hesitate to offer, "The good lady Pritchen with whom I stay has more rooms to let. You will come with me this very evening and explain to your fine cousin that it is a matter of business. You and I must be in the same tavern in order to conduct government affairs efficiently. Surely he cannot argue with your career. Then, the room will be available to a paying man and their pantry will hopefully be plentiful for a time."

Curtis mulled this over for a minute or two. Finally, he agreed the idea was suitable. William led Curtis to one of the round windows and pointed to Mrs. Pritchen's home, just steps from the Capitol. The two old friends tipped their hats and made plans to meet for dinner. William would alert Mrs. Pritchen to Curtis' arrival. When Savannah heard Curtis walk away, she tugged on William's sleeve.

"Is it all clear?"

"Relatively, but stay down. We are going outside; we will chat there.", he directed.

Savannah watched from under the ruffles as the House of Burgesses passed out of sight. They exited the Capitol and William told his pocket there was no reason she couldn't sit in on some of those sessions, too. Inside the great, velvet pocket, Savannah was looking forward to a very full year of government education.

The outside portico, or bottom section of the "bridge", was architecturally perfect to catch strong wind gusts. A big gust swept through walkway and its arches, giving a chill. Savannah wrapped her cloak tightly about her and snuggled deeper in William's pocket. As they parted the building, the sounds of the Capitol shifted. William's walking stick shifted from stone floor to broken oyster shells. Briefly, she heard a flurry of loud and boisterous voices as they, she assumed, passed the Exchange. Then, as William's walking stick clicked further off the grounds, she heard fewer voices. Those she did hear were becoming more and more faint as the crunching of oyster shells under William's boots became more and more dominant.

This was something very Virginian that Savannah noticed at some of the James River plantations. Oysters were so abundant in the nearby rivers that they were a regular part of daily meals. So many oysters were eaten that shells were recycled. The shells would be crushed into tiny pieces and then used for walkways, garden paths, entryways or any outdoor area where surfacing was needed. She peered out of his pocket and looked at the trees she had been considering earlier.

They looked awfully dark and very creepy even in the middle of the day. She heard strange noises in the woods behind the Capitol and, even in daylight, could see nothing between the trees because the woods were so thick. She began to rethink her option of living on Capitol grounds. Certainly, the College trees were just a scary at night, but Bartholomew's tree stood just inside the entrance. At least there, she could have her back to Wren Building and always have a friend very close. Being a city squirrel and used to trees around London, the idea of forested trees was exciting, but just a little too scary. The closer to a building, the better. Even though Williamsburg was the capital and many fine, wealthy and cultured individuals lived on the nearby James River, Virginia was very wild and completely unlike any capital she ever visited in Europe. Even Salzburg was less primitive than this. She heard stories of wolves, panthers and who knows what else lurking in the Virginia wilds. Besides, now that she knew there were pirates and Indians right here in town at the Public Gaol, she knew she couldn't live within eyesight of the gaol. She had never seen an Indian or a pirate and wasn't sure what to expect. Naturally, being a curious squirrel, she would love to meet and talk with a Virginia Indian or a Carolina pirate, just not late at night.

"Are you ready to see your first pirate, Miss Savannah?", William's gentle tone brought her foreboding thoughts of pirates directly into reality.

"Right this minute?", she asked.

Noting they were alone, she ran up his arm and pulled her cloak tighter, more to ward off pirates than the cold.

"Perhaps they are busy and we would be disturbing them."

"Trust me, they are only busy being frightened of what may await them next month. Some of them are very poor souls whom may or may not have committed any crimes, and hopefully evidence, or lack thereof, will set them free. Still, some are very evil and will be judged so and hanged in April."

William could see Savannah was very nervous. Still, he felt it very important for a young, sheltered squirrel to see something like this. Savannah was somewhat spoiled and he hoped by showing her the prison and its prisoners, she might better understand the world and it philosophy. Not everyone was from a wealthy and well-bred family and the sooner she realized that, the better and more compassionate squirrel she would be. Still, he tried to take her mind off the situation for a moment.

"Before we head to the gaol, do you have any questions regarding the workings of the Capitol?"

Happy the conversation had shifted, Savannah broached a wee concern.

"What I have to keep straight in my head is how the General Assembly is divided." Savannah closed her eyes, remembered hard and recited, "The Council is the upper house of the legislature and they are appointed by the Queen and help with the Royal Governor's matters, plus make laws. The House of Burgesses is the lower house of the legislature and gentlemen landowners elect each member and they then elect their own Speaker, or leader. Then, when the two Houses have a disagreement or need to discuss anything at all, they meet in the "bridge" room, also known as the Conference Room which sits between the two Houses."

She opened her eyes and let out a deep breath. That was a lot for a young squirrel to ingest after only one afternoon.

"You have a very fine memory, Miss Savannah. Am I correct in assuming you enjoy the teaching of colonial government and law?"

"Oh, indeed. If I could, I would study law exclusively and become a member of the House of Burgesses one day.", she said excitedly.

"Noble aspirations. Your enthusiasm and precise recall of instruction will come in handy throughout the season as you watch various trials and legislative sessions. Not to mention how it will aid you in your 'secret studies'."

Savannah smiled broadly. She loved being reminded of her intelligence.

"You will also be able to look at the concept of the gaol more intellectually, realizing it too is merely a part of the judicial system of our new government. It is a necessity, a vital part of the whole legislative and court system."

Savannah's smile drooped and she sighed heavily. He tricked her right into going to the gaol. Well, it was best to be done with it. The sooner they visited the gaol, the sooner she could get back to Mrs. Pritchen's and her lovely vegetable gardens.

"Come. You will be perfectly safe. Just stay in my pocket, hide behind the ruffles and try to remember the people you will see are humans, just like me. Some are guilty and some are not.", he opened his pocket. "Are you ready?"

Chapter XIII

Savannah sat very still on his shoulder, unconsciously pulling her cloak tighter to her chest. A bit of sunlight reflected off William's rapier and she realized, of course she'd be safe. After all, wasn't William the Gentleman Slayer? She smiled at William and snuggled deeper into his pocket.

"Could we stop for some lunch first?", she hoped.

"No. I think it would serve as a better lesson were our tummies not satisfied.", he answered emphatically.

Savannah was surprised by this response. William tried to explain as they walked north, past the Main Street and toward the Public Gaol.

"You must remember, some of these men have not eaten full meals in some time. The Assembly provides them with meager sustenance; however, unless they are independently wealthy and are fortunate enough to have someone from the outside to bring them specially requested meals, they subsist mostly on a diet of salt-dried beef and Indian cornmeal."

Savannah felt bad again about being so selfish.

"What have many of these men done to be imprisoned?", she asked sympathetically as they continued walking across the green field between the Capitol and the Gaol.

"Specifically, my Assembly acquaintances tell me of the following.", he began.

In the near distance, a flock of sheep grazed. One bleated, as if encouraging William to continue his lesson.

"There are quite a few men and three women who are awaiting trials which could result in death."

"Oh my! What did these people do to deserve to die?", she gasped.

"The two women are to be judged in the crimes of forgery of financial documents. The men are a mixture of burglars, arsonists, horse thieves and murderers."

"Forgery? Is that truly punishable by death?", Savannah was horrified.

"In most cases, yes. Sometimes the Assembly grants life but administers mutilation or severe lashings that seem to be mutilations in themselves."

Savannah was suddenly very sad and did not want to visit the Gaol.

"I do not wish to visit any longer, Col. Byrd. May we please go home?", she pleaded.

"You know, the Gaol also serves as an educational tool. Do you think the young children who pass by here each day and see the prison conditions know that to commit crimes is wrong? Do you think the children of the gaolers plan to steal or forge anything, ever? It is necessary for us to tour even the sad places of our new capital, Miss Savannah."

Savannah's tummy began to hurt as they came upon the Gaol. Before she could even grasp the architecture, the stench greeted her with a growing strength as they approached the entrance. Human and livestock waste, rotting meat and months of no bathing announced the Public Gaol. An air of malodorous sadness and despair hung over the long, brick building, telling the visitor this was a place of somber and bad things. One would know to venture far from this building, even if one didn't know what it held.

William reminded Savannah to keep low as he ascended the wooden steps and opened the door to enter the office. He saw the keeper and explained he wished to audit the Gaol, just take a look around so he could be well acquainted with all aspects of the capital. Of course, the keeper admitted William, a fine gentleman, to the Gaol. He insisted on escorting William as some of the prisoners were out in the exercise yard. The gaoler put down the ham and bread he was eating which William assumed was prisoners' food, and hurriedly grabbed his ring of keys. Savannah could smell him all the way down in her pocket and wished she had a nice orange and clove pomatum. He unlocked a thick wooden door with the noise that only large cast iron keys and locks can make. Savannah could tell the door was opened wide, not by the sound of it scraping against the hardened dirt floor, but by the wave of wretched odors that were exponentially stronger than they were from the office of the keeper. Savannah heard the same tone of chatter she heard in the Exchange, but could tell by the content of discussion and the harsh, uneducated accents, this was not a meeting of gentlemen.

Inside the gaol, Savannah and William walked through a room that stood between the keeper's area and the exercise yard. William's boots now made a scratchy, matted sound as they tread heavily on what sounded like straw. It was here Savannah finally had to poke out her head and see what was going on. Holding her breath, she looked over the pocket trim at the surroundings.

Indeed, there was straw everywhere. The straw was spread out all over the floor of what looked like a large cell that should hold about six people. There were black, iron shackles chained to the walls, leg irons and some horrible, wooden containers in the corners she assumed were for personal usage. There were dozens of thin, threadbare blankets strewn around the floor and more than a few rats scurrying in and out of the straw. The very straw itself seemed to harbor the essence of the putrid stench that hung in the air. Savannah looked up at William, who was covering his nose with a crisp, white, linen handkerchief. Thinking it a marvelous solution, she grabbed a small section of his ruffle and covered her own nose. Tugging at another section with her free hand, she had a question for William.

"How many prisoners sleep in here?"

William figured it best to let the gaolkeeper answer.

"Good man, how many offenders do you keep in this cell?", he asked for Savannah's benefit.

"Currently, sir, we got thirty-six and expectin' thirteen more soon as the next ship arrives from Barbados: pirates, don't you know.", the gaolkeeper answered with a wink.

Savannah heard a loud chuckle from one of the corners. She fidgeted about in the pocket to see who in this pit had the spirit to actually laugh. When she saw the man, shackled in leg irons to the wall, she felt a shiver travel right up her tail. He was a pirate. He had to be. He looked exactly like the stories she heard as a young squirrel. She knew they existed; it wasn't as though they were legends or fairy tales. They were merely sailors and thieves who sought, trapped and ambushed merchant ships and then robbed them blind. Some were evil and would murder their victims; some were less malicious and would make their victims strip to their bare skin and drop them in the nearest town in that condition. Some, it was rumored, even worked for the Queen herself. They were called privateers and stole from Spanish, French and Portuguese ships. Savannah wondered on which waters this pirate plundered and pillaged. Barbados? North Carolina? Virginia? Haiti?

The pirate looked Col. Byrd up and down, admiring his fine attire, his sparkling clean rapier and Savannah wondered if he would rob William had he the chance. Looking at his sullied, scarlet-cum-rust frock coat, which had obviously been quite fine at one time, she presumed he had torn it from a captain's back. She concluded that he would definitely rob William had he the chance. William though, she was certain, would fight him off in a grand sword fight to the death. Swinging from masts and hanging from sails, William would cut and thrust the entire hoard of privateers left and right until they all jumped into the briny, shark-infested sea, just to escape the Gentleman Slayer.

Savannah giggled to herself and then turned her attention back to the matter at hand.

"Pirates are not so frightening.", she thought valiantly to herself. Still, it was very exciting and she couldn't wait to tell Dante about it tonight.

"I understand you keep five here whom await death trials. Is this man one of them?", William pointed with his walking stick at the pirate.

"Yes, sir. Cap'n Maurice Bloodstone. He's a fierce and relentless marauder who takes human life as easily as the buttons off your frock, sir.", the gaoler said with palpable disdain and the pride that, at the very least, he was morally and socially superior to someone, even if that someone was a pirate.

"Of what crime is he accused?"

"Mass murder, sir. The story goes he and his crew boarded a merchant ship headed to Jamestown from the West Indies. His intent was to take the cargo of silks and spices, all gathered on journeys to the Far East. Once on board, he ordered his henchmen to kill all the men on the ship and for each man to choose a bride from the wenches aboard. Then, them wenches what wasn't taken were made to walk the plank after the men. In all fifty-six men and women were fed to the Carolina sharks. He was captured when one of his own murdering men turned in his whereabouts for the reward. Strange thing of it, sir, was that the squealer was staying in the same village near the Carolina-Virginia border as Cap'n. Bloodstone. Got hisself captured in the process! Already been hanged along with three of his friends. The Cap'n is the last one to die. Can't come soon enough if you ask me, murdering women is unspeakable. Wouldn't be surprised if the trial shows up in 'The Boston News-Letter' this summer.", the gaoler walked over to the pirate and spat on his coat. The pirate just laughed.

"It shall be ye who die, gaolkeeper, sir! I'll cut you and your family to pieces before they hang me! Haaaaa-haaaaaa!", he laughed an eerie and purely evil laugh that made Savannah shudder.

William patted her head through his ruffle, making her feel very safe. William refused to fuel the pirate's antagonistic demeanor and chose to ignore him, as though he was a non-subject.

"Who are the others you keep?", he asked the gaoler, turning in a most dignified manner away from the pirate.

"Well, sir, we got a number of slaves what just arrived by ship. They's to be kept here until ready for sale.

We also got some convicts what London didn't want no more. They come here instead of being hanged back in England, sir.", he said proudly, kicking a young English man shackled to a wall.

"Who is that young man you just stepped upon?", William stressed the word 'stepped' with sarcasm and eyed the gaolkeeper knowingly.

Wiping some dried food off his face, the gaolkeeper answered, "Oh, this young man, sir? Sorry about that, sir. I must have not seen him. Name's Daniel Mullaly. He come by way of Philadelphia, but stinks of pure Irish trash. He agreed to seven years of indentured servitude to a silversmith up north. Got his passage paid for from Dublin, then got here and took off running. His owner said there won't be no charges pressed, long as we hold him 'til he come to get him. Should be gone by next week."

The young Irishman looked up at William and smiled weakly, his mouth completely rotted and black. His eyes looked worn and spoke of a hard life for such youth. There was no spirit inside and William felt sorry for him. William squatted to the prisoner's level. This was extremely uncommon for someone of William's social standing. To be in a place like this was odd in itself, but to actually bend down and talk to a prisoner was scandalous.

"Why did you run away, Daniel?", he asked softly, reserving judgment.

Daniel's green eyes averted William's and instead watched a rat run across the floor and into the hay where another prisoner would be sleeping tonight.

"Do not be scared, Daniel. I am merely curious. A gentleman pays for your passage and you do not honor your deal. You do not strike me as a boy who would do so without provocation. Why, Daniel?"

Daniel still didn't speak. Slowly though, with the great weight and clatter of heavy chains, he pushed aside his matted, shoulder-length, red hair to reveal the vacant space where an ear should have been. William was horrified.

"Did your owner remove your ear, Daniel?", William asked, his voice quivering with fury.

Daniel nodded and responded with a hearty Irish brogue, "Yes, sir. He caught me listening to a conversation he was having with a fellow from the town. They was talking about racehorses, sir.", Daniel's eyes became fluid. "I took care of a horse back in Dublin, sir. I think maybe someday I will have enough money to buy my own fine horse here in America. I only wanted to learn more about horses. He tells me I was disrespectful and would teach me to never listen again to something that didn't concern me, sir. So, he cut off my ear and I ran away that night."

William was fuming. He owned slaves and indentures servants himself, but never treated them with such disregard and malice. It was unbelievable that one human being could do such a thing to another. William began to stand. As he did so, Daniel caught a glimpse of Savannah. They locked tear-filled eyes and Savannah wished she had never come to the gaol. Daniel smiled slightly at Savannah, the only pleasurable thing he'd seen in weeks.

William turned to the gaoler, "I do not want this boy released to his owner."

"But, sir, I cannot. His owner is his owner. He will take him when he comes."

Taking out a leather pocketbook, William wrote his name and Mrs. Pritchen's address on a piece of paper. He then took a remarkable stack of bank notes out of a section of the pocketbook and handed it all to the gaoler.

"You will give this money to the boy's owner along with my information. Should the funds not be sufficient to buy another servant, I will expect a visit. However, I am certain that amount is more than a silversmith can make in an entire year's time. He will be satisfied.", he directed the gaolkeeper, who eyed the money hungrily. "And good man, " William continued, "I will know if the monies were not received; for I expect when he arrives to find no servant and no compensation, he will easily slit your throat as he did the boy's ear."

The gaolkeeper gulped loudly.

"I will also know if you kept any portion of the monies for yourself. For, have you heard the legend of the Gentleman Slayer?"

"Aye, sir, I have. My own daughter has been telling tales late at night, just to scare the little son of the family.", he laughed ignorantly.

"Did she tell of his black curls and silver rapier?", William toyed with the man, feigning to draw his rapier from its sheath.

The gaoler stopped mid-laugh as William's curls and the glint of his sword caught his eyes. He stared at William with eyes wide as coins.

"That is correct, gaolkeeper,", William said authoritatively, "lest you wish to wake to the shock of cold steel to flesh, I suggest you keep our deal honorable. Am I understood?"

The gaolkeeper nodded quickly and silently.

"Good. Now, here is something for your honor. I trust it will buy suitable shoes for those children of yours.", he handed the man more money, folded to easily fit a pocket.

"Thank you, sir, thank you. I am sure Mr. Bernard will find the sum more than enough. I will send him to your lodging should he be unhappy. Of course,", he said with a wink and a nervous laugh, "he probably won't want to meet in the night with the Gentleman Slayer either."

Savannah was amazed at all the business being transacted. Besides that, she was thrilled their story was making such rounds. It was even being used in situations she would never have guessed. She couldn't wait to tell Dante and the others at the graveyard tonight.

"Daniel,", William said kindly, "how would you like to come work for me? I have a number of racehorses that need care and brooding mares ready to give birth at any time."

Daniel was speechless. William instructed the gaoler to unlock Daniel's shackles and they would be back inside in a few moments. He wanted Daniel ready to leave with them when they returned. With that, he walked out into the exercise yard to continue Savannah's lesson.

The stench in the cell merely stretched out to the yard. The proliferation of fresh air had no effect on it and William and Savannah continued to cover their noses with linen and lace. Savannah saw the two women William had mentioned. They were barely recognizable from the men. All had long, filthy hair that could have been blonde or brunette, but one couldn't truly tell due to the ancient dirt. They all looked very thin, with great black hollows below their eyes and in their cheeks. William told Savannah that sometimes, if a prisoner had some funds on the outside, he would be allowed to have a relative bring food and drink and clothing from the outside into the prison. Perhaps some of those men of means were in here today, but Savannah couldn't distinguish them if there were. Then, she saw a group of men who looked so different from any human she'd ever seen she had to ask William what they were.

They weren't Irish, they weren't Spanish even. Their skin was dark and red, like the clay that paved the roads traveled around the South. They had beautiful skin still: smooth, flawless clay, not like the pockmarked and sickly pale skin of much of the English aristocracy, ruined by years of zinc, talc, paint and makeup. These men had high, prominent bones in their faces that made them look like sculptures she had seen during her studies in Florence.

Most interestingly, considering their deplorable conditions, they appeared stoic, proud and remarkably well kept. Another point of interest she noticed, was that they all wore the same greatcoats. Most exciting though, was their other attire.

Long, leather trousers were something she had never seen, but here they were. Each man wore a form of loose leather pant through which skin showed. Savannah thought this was most lacking in decorum and probably very chilly. They had bare feet and, oddly enough, wore feathers around their necks, ears and heads. Savannah was just beside herself with curiosity. Were these the fabled Indians of whom she'd heard so much? She tugged at William's coat again and urged him to ask more questions on her behalf.

"Who are these Indian men, gaoler?"

"So these are Indians!", she thought gleefully to herself. She felt rather bad for them actually. With their unsmiling, composed, unflappable expressions, they looked far too dignified to have done anything seriously wrong, especially when she looked around at their prison mates.

"Don't know much about them, sir. Brought in the winter of last year, I do know. Been here over at least four months now.", he said, leering at them as though he fancied he was superior to yet someone else.

"Yes, I do recall talk of these Indians. The Assembly took great interest in their care. Those greatcoats they all wear were supplied to them by the Assembly as winters in Virginia can go from pleasant to brutal without fair notice. If correct, I believe their trials involve accusations of marauding the villages of our fair Virginia.", William searched his mental notes.

Once back inside the gaol, William demanded of the gaoler Daniel's belongings; there was only a knapsack, empty of all except a dirtied, muslin shirt and round piece of leather, tied with string to make a coin holder. The leather piece was void of any coin and William suspected the gaoler was now a few schillings wealthier. Never mind, William would allow the boy some schillings of his own once in a while.

Of course, Daniel would not be paid for his equestrian services. He would work off the equivalent of his overseas passage. In short, seven years of unpaid labor. Still, he would now be able to work with horses, live in safe quarters, certain that his new owner would not harm him, that is unless he tried to run from Westover. William Byrd II was known to be almost mercifully indifferent to his servants and staff, white and black. Generally, he left them alone, made little or no mention of them in conversation and provided them with, by colonial standards, plenty of sustenance and sufficient shelter. However, he was known to punish as he deemed necessary. Tales were told of his runaway slaves. Tales were vivid enough that not many of them ran away. Besides, after the kindness William showed to an insignificant, Irish refugee, such disloyalty would be attended to with severity.

When William felt Savannah had gleaned enough reality for one afternoon, he took charge of Daniel, bowed his head with a barely noticeable tilt, and bid the gaoler a questionably good afternoon. The gaoler held the door open for William, allowed him enough room to pass and then let the heavy door slam just before Daniel's face. Uttering some poorly enunciated and rude exchanges, the former prisoner and his gaoler bid each other a good afternoon.

Daniel fell into line behind William. He walked with his head down, but his eyes up, darting them back and forth as he checked out his new home of Virginia. On quick judgment, he deemed it much greener than Philadelphia, but that was nothing new. After all, he was from Ireland, the Emerald Isle, named so for its own verdant landscape. He liked the trees, not many like these in Ireland, but he noticed the town to be a little unpolished, at least compared to Philadelphia. Philadelphia's roads and towns were flocked with people and carriages. There appeared to be more livestock than humans in these streets. Nevertheless, it struck him as a nice place and the bucolic atmosphere might prove to be just the thing for a young Irish boy who, weeks ago, had begun wondering if he hadn't made a horrible mistake in coming to America.

Chapter XIV

Daniel sniffed the air as Mrs. Pritchen opened the front door. A waft of seasoned oysters greeted the newest boarder at the door. The thought of a dinner consisting of anything other than aged, dried beef caused instant pangs in Daniel's concave stomach.

"Who is this young man?", Mrs. Pritchen asked, making no effort to disguise her affront to Daniel's foul odor.

"I would like to introduce Daniel Mullaly. He will be joining my staff as a groom, caring for my prized racehorses.", he shot his cuffs and smiled conservatively at Daniel.

"Well, I hope you know your horses, young Mullaly. There are plenty a boy in the whole of Virginia who would be honored to have the opportunity to care for the Byrd equines.", she said curtly.

Mrs. Pritchen was a mere tavern owner, but had been exposed to the gentility and refinement of the colonial gentry from Massachusetts down the Atlantic to Virginia. She assumed power and prestige by the company she kept, even if they were boarders first, friends second. A ragged, awful-smelling boy, Irish no less, was certainly not worthy of her attention. However, she was a servant of William's and she silently agreed to herself to afford at least the same amount of respect as did he. Daniel seemed to know what she was thinking and tried his best to contain his odor, as if keeping his arms tightly pressed to his sides would curtail weeks of prison contamination.

"We've got to get you outside and washed up. You can't stand in my house smelling like barnyard waste. Go out the back door and look to the left. You'll see a large wooden barrel in a shed. You can get water from the well behind the shed. Don't you start complaining about how cold the water is. Just clean yourself quickly and get yourself back indoors. I'll find some clean trousers and shirt for you and set them on the tree stump outside the shed door. Dinner's in two hours. I'm going to need some help with cooking. You'd best check with your master to see if he's got chores for you to do; if not, come back to the kitchen when you're clean.", she directed, pushing him through the house toward the back door.

His eyes caught a hunk of salt pork as she walked him through the kitchen. Mrs. Pritchen's eyes caught the hunger in those eyes. She wasn't completely without compassion. Seeing his desperation, she grabbed a small piece of the pork and some nearby bread.

"Here, eat it slowly or you'll make yourself sick; I won't have my perfectly good food be thrown back up by an urchin who has the table manners of a goat.", she put the food in his hand and gave him a final shove out the back door and pointed to the shed at the left.

William spent the couple of hours before dinner in Mrs. Pritchen's library. For a tavern owner, she had a relatively large library of about fifty books. Even some of the intellectuals of the landed gentry only owned a few hundred books or less. She had the staples: the King James bible, Shakespeare, Chaucer, Plato, Socrates, and Spenser. In need of something lighthearted, considering the Daniel incident and what awaited William tomorrow morning, he chose a copy of Shakespeare's "Twelfth Night, Or What You Will". The plot involving mistaken identity and ridiculous confusion seemed apropos as he pondered the legend of the Gentleman Slayer. Perhaps it was all mistaken identity. As he read a page of silly banter betwixt Viola disguised as the boy-page Cesario and the love-struck Lady Olivia over and over without remembering what he had read, he found himself thinking more and more about tomorrow's duel. Could the Slayer and the duel be connected? He set down his book and lit a long, clay pipe filled with Virginia tobacco. Sitting back in the well-worn, wing chair, he thought hard with each puff of his pipe.

Finally, the only thing he could think of was that Rolly had become intoxicated on too much claret and had begun bragging about the duel. At that point, he surmised, someone who knew William had spoken in his defense, even exaggerating to counteract the babbling bravado of a drunken duelist. Most likely, an eavesdropper heard the story, retold it to another gentleman who retold it to a barmaid who retold it her daughter who retold it to a friend and so on and so on until it finally reached William. Two days doesn't seem like enough time for a legend to be created, but rumors, especially ghastly ones involving bloodlust were popular and could fly through this colony like a hurricane.

He looked at the small clock on the fireplace mantle and noted it would soon be time to dine. He insisted Daniel take the free time after he bathed and enjoy some coffee whilst helping Mrs. Pritchen with dinner. William also insisted that Daniel partake in the meal with everyone at the dining room table. Mrs. Pritchen just about passed out at this suggestion. She had never known a servant to dine with the gentry and severely disliked the idea of it happening at her table. Nevertheless, she held her tongue and understood her place; she was the tavern owner and Col. Byrd was the wealthy plantation owner in town on high business. If he wanted to invite an Irish goat to sit at the table, she would oblige.

Savannah had spent the last two hours in the kitchen, talking with Mrs. Pritchen and getting to know Daniel. He was a little surprised to shake hands with a talking squirrel, but after a few moments he forgot she was a squirrel. She was so eloquent and intelligent, he didn't care whether she was a human, a sheep, a cow or a salmon. She was kind and interesting company and that was all he cared about this night.

Dinner looked as tasty as Daniel had hoped. Helping Mrs. Pritchen serve was about the most difficult thing he could have been asked to do this evening. Plowing a wheat field with his bare hands would have been easier than serving steaming Brunswick stew, Welsh rabbit, fried chicken and Virginia game pie before he was allowed to eat. The hearty bread alone was enough to make his stomach growl. Fortunately, he had eaten that salt pork sandwich earlier, otherwise his stomach growls may have scared the livestock outside on the Main Street.

When everyone was served, Daniel was asked to join the table. The rest of the boarders found it highly unusual to have a servant at the table. Still, being the gentlemen they were and knowing this was an odd wish of Col. Byrd, they went to great lengths to hide their disdain. Monsieur LeVau and Mr. Gilbert exchanged glances as if to say, "Good heavens!". Yet, no one questioned the actions or sentiments of William. Just as Savannah had been intellectually stimulating enough to cause Daniel to forget she was a squirrel, the fine gentlemen of the table eventually discovered that Daniel and his story were intriguing enough to cause them to forget he was a servant. As it turned out, Daniel was quite intelligent and, although not classically educated, was the recipient of remarkable education for a rural Irish boy. His mother was a sculptress who visited Florence and Rome and Paris in the early years of her first marriage. Her first husband was a wealthy silk merchant who took her on all his travels. Sadly, he died mysteriously in his sleep one night. His family, thinking she poisoned him, sued for her inheritance, a modest fortune, won and left her destitute. She went back to Dublin, married a struggling wheat farmer and gave birth to Daniel a year later. Her life turned harsh, as though her days of travel and sculpting had only been a dream. Still, she retained her world schooling and passed it on to Daniel when he wasn't working the earth. He knew who Canaletto, Bernini and Botticelli were and the architectural differences between Notre Dame and Chartres Cathedrales. When Daniel was in his eleventh year, his parents died in a carriage accident. He spent the next seven years scraping a meal and a bed here and there by working on various farms and grooming what horses he could. Finally, one day he decided to take advantage of the indentured servitude concept and next thing he knew, he was in America, lost and ear, ended up in prison and now he was here.

Daniel stated his story very matter-of-factly and very succinctly without emotion. When he was done, he turned his face back toward his cabbage and butter salad and finished his meal quietly, leaving the others to regain conversations and fill the tavern with elegant laughter and speeches.

When dinner was finished, Monsieur LeVau, Mr. Gilbert and William sat in the library drinking brandy while they discussed Capitol business and smoked Virginia tobacco from their long pipes. Daniel helped Mrs. Pritchen clean the dishes and ready the morning's breakfast. Savannah and Dante waited impatiently in the herb garden for bedtime and the eventual midnight meeting. They were already sharing stories they heard; Savannah told him all about how Rolly ran scared past William at the Capitol. They both heard people of all sorts telling the legend throughout the day: Savannah the various men at the Capitol and Dante, the merchants gossiping with goodewives.

Finally, it was time to go to bed. William excused himself to practice some fencing and read his latest copy of "The Boston News-Letter". Savannah wanted to tell him not to worry about the fencing, for it looked as though he wouldn't need it. Remarkably, William appeared unaffected by tomorrow's early duel. Perhaps he knew Rolly would back out, all talk, all coward. Nevertheless, Savannah was still nervous and would feel much better after the graveyard meeting. Once she knew the story had done its job thoroughly, she would feel much better. She looked at the small mantle clock in the bedroom and sighed heavily. It was only eight-thirty.

Savannah slept restlessly for a couple of hours and waited for Dante's secret knock. Finally, *tap-tap-tap* and *whoosh-whoosh* announced the midnight hour. She recognized his claw taps and tail whooshes instantly. She looked up toward William's bed and saw it was empty. Most likely, he was still downstairs with LeVau and

Gilbert. William enjoyed staying up very late discussing politics and philosophy and drinking wine. Even with such a day ahead, he would still join them for a pipe. He probably fenced for a bit and returned to the library.

Savannah and Dante tiptoed downstairs, each leaping quietly over the fourth, creaky step. Landing with the silent thud of eight padded paws, the two devious mates stood frozen, making sure no one was watching. After checking all directions, they looked at each other, nodded and ran for the back door. Sure enough, as they passed the library, they heard William pontificating loudly about someone Greek. Savannah assumed it was Plato, for as she passed, she heard him ask, "What is justice?"

Outside in the cold spring air, Dante and Savannah checked their hats and cloaks in the herb garden. Making sure her cloak was fastened and her gloves on securely, Savannah pulled her ruffled cap over her sharp ears. There was a nippy breeze and her ears were always more susceptible than the rest of her body. Dante straightened the feathers in his velvet tricorn. He had worn all black for tonight's meeting. Being a very melodramatic cat, he thought the simple velvet cloak and hat would be most thespian for a graveyard meeting. His frock coat and breeches were of a deep, rich scarlet. Proud of his ensemble, Dante turned to Savannah and asked, "Are you ready for a scare?"

She nodded in the affirmative and just as the two were turning to leave, the door creaked slowly. Someone was coming outside.

Standing in the doorway, splendidly dressed in black velvet himself, Ichabod tapped his mahogany, silver-capped walking stick three times and announced his intentions in his commanding, Teutonic accent.

"I do hope your graveyard rendezvous has room for one more. I love a good scheme."

"You know about. . .the uh. . .,", Savannah stammered.

"About 'the plan'? Of course, my dear. When one has been a member of the finest courts of Europe, one knows how to keep one's ears open and one's mouth shut."

Dante mimicked Ichabod as he spoke to Savannah. Ichabod turned at the last moment and caught Dante mid-mimic. Dante covered himself by pretending to be cleaning his whiskers with his paws. Ichabod smiled smugly and turned back to Savannah.

"Now, shall we?", he bent deeply at the waist and swept his huge gold-buttoned cuff across the air, making an invisible path for Savannah.

Not to be outdone, Dante also swept an imaginary path. Dressed in almost identical black cloaks, hats and gloves, Ichabod and Dante looked like cast iron bookends, waiting for the complete works of Shakespeare. Savannah curtsied to both and walked the oyster shell path that led out of the gardens and through the wooden fence. Dante and Ichabod followed, each attempting supreme gentility, offering first passage to the other until, tired of watching the silly charade, Savannah walked back and pulled each one through the gate and the three headed onto the Main Street an into the black Virginia night.

Chapter XV

As if it was stage design from a Scottish tragedy, the Bruton Parish graveyard was cold, moist and shrouded in a low fog, low enough to allow the tops of the tombstones to peek above the eerie mist. The three friends' excitement quickly abated as they neared the graveyard. Ichabod and Dante, each determined to be the braver, kept pace with each other until they reached the edge where the street and the churchyard met. They looked at each other, bowing over and over again to allow the other entrance first. Savannah quickly became tired of waiting and pushed past the both of them.

"Come along, you two. We shall all be safe if we stick together.", she soothed her friends, trying to mask her own fear.

"I do not see any of your friends.", acknowledged Ichabod in a quite tone.

"They are about.", Dante assured him, looking at the treetops, listening for familiar voices.

At that moment, there was a loud rustling coming from an overgrown magnolia tree. The flowers that hung near the bottom rustled momentarily. The three adventurers stopped mid-step and pivoted toward the noise. It was a large rustling, presumably made by a large creature.

"Are your feline relatives of the mammoth size, dear Dante?", asked Ichabod, drawing his rapier, unsheathing it halfway.

"Only Grandma Pernod, but she's up in New Jersey.", he said nervously, also drawing his rapier.

"Shhhhh!", demanded Savannah.

The noise grew closer and more formidable. As it did so, there came with it a great and awful smell. Savannah froze in terror. She knew that smell. Savannah began to back up, very slowly. Dante and Ichabod watched her and absorbed her fright as they watched her face. Certain that something capable of such ruckus and such odor could only be a detriment to their health, the three continued to work their way backwards to the Street. Then, with a great leap, the creature emerged from behind the magnolia. It was Petruchio.

"Run!", Savannah screamed as Petruchio lunged for her.

"Stop, please. I mean no harm to you or your friends.", the great beast pleaded.

Savannah stopped, twisting her head toward the voice. It was a strong accent, not of Virginia or England. It

wasn't French and it wasn't German like Ichabod's.
Quickly, she scanned her memory for any other time in her
life she had heard an accent such as this. There it was: a
former Italian tutor back in London. The accent was Italian.
She turned her body to line up with her head and looked
Petruchio right in his great yellow eyes. Looking closer, she
realized they were not yellow at all; they were brown.
Petruchio's eyes were softly brown.

"What do you want from us?", she demanded of
Petruchio, Dante and Ichabod standing behind her, swords
drawn but trembling.

"I want only to say Hello. I have been trying to meet
you since we were shipmates. I saw you at the College and
on the Street a number of times but you always seemed so
scared."

Dante and Savannah stared at each other. They
could not believe what they were hearing. Remembering
little Bartholomew, Dante was certain it was a trick. From
behind Savannah's skirt, he waggled his sword in
Petruchio's directions and questioned his sincerity.

"We do not believe you, sir. What about my friend
Bartholomew? He is still recovering from your great
mouth."

"I am sorry to hear of this. Many a day have passed when I wished to visit him, but I cannot get near enough with his new treetop bedroom.", Petruchio explained solemnly.

"I saw you carry him down the Street! I rescued him by landing on your back!"

"This I recall. You are a brave friend.", Petruchio bowed to Dante.

Dante became braver and stepped to Savannah's side.

"You must know I was carrying Bartholomew to the side of a peruke-maker's shop. I had seen him exit a hole in that wall one day and assumed it was his house.", he explained further.

"Why were you carrying him in your mouth?", Dante's tone became softer.

"It was the quickest thing to do. I was walking through town one afternoon and saw a giant hawk circling above the ground. When I looked at the area it was covering, I saw Bartholomew leaving the cheese maker's shop with a chunk of cheese.", Petruchio told the story with high drama but true modesty.

The three friends stared at Petruchio with amazement. Dante and Ichabod had become so rapt in attention that their swords had dropped to their sides and lay in the grass.

"The next thing I knew, the hawk was diving for Bartholomew. All I could do was to pick up your friend in my mouth and carry him home, where he could be safe."

Savannah didn't know what to say. Then, she remembered the ship and very quickly thought of something to say.

"What about the way you treated all those poor people on the ship? They way you barked at them all the time? What about me? You frightened me half to death, snooping around my quarters. Who were you trying to save then?!", Savannah queried as though she were a member of the General Court, certain she had caught him lying.

"I was not trying to scare the passengers, though I fear I did. I was asking for help. Living with Rolly is horrible and I was asking anyone who would listen to save me from Rolly and adopt me.", Petruchio's eyes glanced downward, filled with tears he didn't want his new friends to see.

"What about me?", Savannah continued, sorry she had to. "Why did you try to scare me?"

"Once again, I was not trying to scare you. I wanted a friend and hoped you might be interested."

Savannah, Dante and Ichabod stood in silence looking at Petruchio. No one knew how to proceed. It was obvious Petruchio had been mistaken for the dog he was not. Savannah felt for him. Just as people assumed she was a pest because she was a squirrel, they had assumed Petruchio was malicious because he was a large Mastiff with bad breath. Ichabod, being the least connected to Petruchio, stepped up to the great dog twenty times his size and invited him to the rendezvous.

"That is why I am here!", Petruchio said happily. "I know of your plan. The hogs and horses behind the Capitol have been speaking of the legend all day and night. I asked one of the hogs about it; he told me of this rendezvous he heard from a farm cat. This duel is ridiculous. Everything your fine friend Col. Byrd said that day at the College was true. I want to help anyway I can.", he begged.

Savannah walked over to Petruchio and scampered up to sit on his head.

"I believe we can use your help, Petruchio. Let us find the rest of our friends, friend."

Petruchio smiled, exposing his large, yellow and smelly teeth. Savannah thought perhaps Mrs. Pritchen had some herbs in her garden that might help that affliction. Petruchio sat on his hindquarters to allow Dante and

Ichabod to hop on his back. Like an African elephant, he lumbered with a modicum of grace to the back section of the graveyard, carrying his three new friends.

Bartholomew saw Petruchio joining the gathering and nearly fainted. Yet, after Petruchio explained to Bartholomew what really happened that fateful day last month, Bartholomew was able to relax. Actually, he had chosen a soft spot next to Petruchio's ear into which he nestled perfectly. Initially, when Petruchio and his three companions found the meeting place in the graveyard, the other creatures had scattered into the bushes and low-lying magnolia branches. Poor Petruchio, everyone had only heard gossip and assumptions about his personality and never gave him a chance to prove himself a worthy friend. Yet, after the Bartholomew story and hearing of his wretched treatment by Sir Rolly, the other animals found him to be lovable, generous and strangely gentle for such a large beast.

Before the meeting commenced, a number of the members passed around small, pewter platters of gingerbread and tarts. Mrs. Kinsley, a stout badger made the tarts that morning. Proudly, her son Ignatius offered one to each member.

"These are the best jam tarts you'll ever eat. Take one! My mom's the best baking badger in the whole Virginia colony.", Ignatius bragged loudly.

Mr. Monaghan, an elderly and thin fox made the gingerbread. He was too old to run in the fields with the harriers and beagles anymore, but he did enjoy baking and spent an awful lot of his time trying new recipes. As his granddaughter, Kathleen, walked the large circle, offering a piece to everyone, Mr. Monaghan informed everyone that the gingerbread was a new recipe he'd heard about from a nearby tobacco plantation.

Miss Onyx Treacle, the beautiful rabbit daughter of the widower Gen. Corbin Alistair, poured freshly pressed, hot cider into everyone's tankards.

The larger animals who stood at the back of the circle, the horses, sheep, pigs and Molly, the Jersey cow, had been so busy grazing and eating magnolia leaves that they declined graciously the offers of treats. Actually, this came as quite a relief to Mr. Monaghan. He was pretty certain he hadn't made enough gingerbread for an entire family of pigs.

Everyone chatted quietly and lively about family, the day's events and complimenting the bakers on their confections. There were some conspicuous sounds of enjoyed grazing coming from the Landry pigs and Miss Molly, but other than that, it was as peaceful and relaxing as a gathering could possibly be in a graveyard at midnight. Fog shrouded everyone's view of the street and the rest of the town's buildings. From their points of view, they may as well have been meeting on a graveyard cloud.

After the gingerbread had been consumed, the tarts devoured and cider drained, Savannah decided it was time to get things going. She was anxious to learn of the plan's progression.

"All right friends, new and old alike, who has stories to tell? Who has hopeful news for us that our plan is working as we speak?", Savannah called the meeting to order.

"Tell them what you told me earlier.", Dante urged Savannah. "You know, about Rolly running off outside the Capitol."

Savannah relayed the incident with gravity and seriousness. Petruchio added that he had tried to bark, "Good work!", at Savannah as Rolly ran by, but he was pulling his collar so tightly that Petruchio couldn't get a strong bark going.

"I heard something extremely promising this afternoon.", offered up Ichabod, his strong German accent catching some of the listeners off-guard.

Dante only had time to introduce Ichabod to a few animals the day he arrived. For the most part, he hadn't met very much of the animal community at all. So, Savannah made a general, brief and proper introduction to the group before Ichabod began his tale. Ichabod bowed deeply and placed one booted paw upon a felled branch. He leaned over, rested his forearm over his knee and began to speak dramatically. Dante rolled his eyes.

"I was with Herr LeVau in the Market Square late this morning. He had very important business at the Capitol today and felt perhaps some fresh café would spirit him through his day of political and business commitments.", he stopped to emphasize the importance of his master's day, allowing those of less important homes to digest this information.

He glanced at a spot on his cape, brushed it off, then, with great flair, threw his cape over one shoulder and continued his story. Dante shifted from foot to foot, sighing loudly. Ichabod glanced with raised eyebrows at Dante and turned back to his audience.

"So, there we are walking to Anthony's tea and café stall when who is standing there first, but Sir Roland Grahame himself. Well, I do not have to tell you I was most eager to know of their conversation. Actually, it was not a proper conversation. For, as you know, Rolly would never deign to speak with Anthony. I like that man, Anthony. Very kind. Very kind."

He looked at Mr. Monaghan who nodded in concurrence.

"*Achso*, to continue, it was Anthony who was doing all the talking. He was going on and on, telling Rolly what a fabulous and skilled swordsman he must be. Rolly puffed up his great chest and belly and enjoyed his praise immensely until Anthony told him he thought anybody who would duel with the Gentleman Slayer had to be amazing. Surely he knew he could die if he was not. It was at this point that Rolly turned even paler than his usual shade of flour white. Indeed, said Anthony, the Gentleman Slayer had never lost a duel and never left a victim with his head intact. With this news, Sir Rolly called Anthony insolent for daring to speak to nobility with such disrespect and impertinence."

Ichabod stood upright, placed his hat upon his head and straightened the fingers of his gloves as he finished his recollection.

"With that, Rolly yanked on poor Petruchio's leash and dragged him out of Market Square faster that Rolly's heels could carry him."

Ichabod walked back to his place in the circle and looked at Petruchio.

"I imagine you can verify all of this, dear boy.", he inquired of Petruchio.

Petruchio nodded vigorously, happy to help and always pleased to hear stories that made Rolly sound stupid. A number of others told stories very similar to Ichabod's. Most revolved around one of two points. Either someone was telling Rolly how brave he was to face the Gentleman Slayer and scaring him out of his wits or Rolly overheard someone telling someone else the legend itself. This latter scenario seemed to scare Rolly more than anything. The more tales and preternatural myths he heard about Col. William Byrd II, the Gentleman Slayer, the more frightened and nervous he became.

Finally, as the meeting was winding down and everyone was congratulating each other on the fine work they had done and how they couldn't have done it without the help of the children and gossiping nature of the adults, Petruchio asked Savannah if he could address the group. He had very important news that would make everyone happy. He had been so nervous about speaking aloud, that it had taken him all night to get up the courage to address the members. He was very shy for such a big dog and this endeared him more than anything to his new friends. He spoke in a voice so quiet and timid that everyone had to be completely silent and lean forward to hear him.

"The reason I ran away from home tonight is that, at least I gather by various clues, that Rolly is planning to be on the Grand Anne tomorrow morning. I do not wish to return to London. I like it here in Virginia. There is plenty of room, so many new friends and lots of trees.", he said with a slight blush.

Everybody laughed at his joke and Petruchio suddenly felt more relaxed.

"I saw one of his slaves packing a great sea chest and setting out Rolly's very best frock. Besides, Rolly gets very seasick. In preparation for a voyage, he never eats the night before a sail. I noticed the only thing he had tonight was tea. That is very unlike him, unless he has a belly ache, which could be the case.", he finished reporting.

Petruchio apologized for not knowing more and stepped back into his spot in the circle and smiled nervously at Savannah, asking with his eyes if he had done well. She smiled that he had. Everyone cheered quietly and congratulated each other all over again after Petruchio's news. Savannah, always playing the devil's advocate, reminded all that nothing was certain until the ship sailed and Col. Byrd was safe. Stifling their giggles and good cheer very poorly, everyone nodded in agreement with Savannah and tried to look serious.

With that, the animal families made their separate ways. Miss Onyx Treacle waved demurely to Ichabod who bowed deeply in response. He was the most elegant dog she had ever seen, so continental. Miss Onyx took her father's arm and, looking shyly over her shoulder, watched Ichabod watching her as she led her father back to their hutch behind the Capitol. Mr. Monaghan and Kathleen ran, the elder doing his best to keep up, back to their home at the College; and Ignatius, Mr. and Mrs. Kinsley waddled happily back to their home underneath one of the taverns. The livestock meandered back to their grassy areas in Market Square, talking and wondering about tomorrow all the way.

Savannah, Dante and Ichabod looked at one another after the crowd had cleared. What about Petruchio? He had nowhere to go. He looked sadly at Dante.

"I'll take care of it.", said Dante confidently. "Mrs. Pritchen loves dogs. Truth be known, she has even commented on your great strength and beauty, Petruchio. She always said Rolly didn't deserve such a regal beast."

Petruchio just about died from blushing and looked down at his paws, unable to say anything. Certain that Mrs. Pritchen would be thrilled to have a new pet, the three small friends hopped upon Petruchio's back once again and the elephant lumbered elegantly and happily down the Main Street, toward his new, safe and loving home.

Chapter XVI

The morning promised to be chilly and somber. William had awakened early and had chosen from his trunk the most fanciful and stylish ensemble he had with him. Decidedly a melancholy occasion, William had selected muted and tastefully appropriate colors. Now, standing majestically under a regal oak, he too looked regal in his black silk ensemble. The frock lapels were trimmed with exquisite embroidery of gold and scarlet thread. Underneath this, he wore his finest blouse of silk, its stock and ruffles shimmering as white and fresh as the morning fog shrouding the anxious, grassy knoll. His waistcoat was designed identically to his coat and his breeches were solid black silk. Just below his black-stockinged knees stemmed highly polished, black boots. Finally, on the side of each boot glistened a diamond buckle in the shape of a crown. He looked splendid and he knew it. Savannah thought if anyone looked like the Gentleman Slayer, it was William.

Standing quietly in the mist, Savannah asked William if he was at all frightened.

"No, my dear. I am not. For this is a gentlemen's agreement into which I entered of my own accord. It will be a fair fight and the better man will endure.", he replied with true calm and not a quiver of apprehension.

"Besides,", he continued, leaning close to Savannah who was sitting in his pocket, "I believe I am the better man." He said this with a wink and a wicked smile.

Savannah did not need much reassurance; she knew Rolly would not show. Everyone except William knew Rolly would not show. By all accounts, Rolly was already aboard the Grand Anne and would soon be setting his sails for London.

Savannah surveyed the battlefield as it waited quietly for the macabre meeting of the privileged class. The grass was white with dew, marked only by the lines of footprints left by the two gentlemen present: William and his acting-second, Mr. Curtis Gilbert. Mr. Gilbert stood dressed completely in black, covered in a black cape and black tricorn. On a tree stump next to him, rested a long and deeply hued mahogany box. The box was open, its tiny gold latch freed for the time being. Inside, it was lined with red silk and held with all majesty and decorum William's rapier. It was a fine weapon with a hilt of scrolled silver. The padding within the hilt was red velvet. William waited patiently for Rolly to appear.

"Should you not take this time to practice?", she asked, trying to throw him off the fact that Rolly was not going to show.

"That is unnecessary. If I am not ready at this moment, I will never be so. First and foremost though, it is considered very bad form to draw your weapon before your opponent arrives."

Wishing she could tell him, Savannah just kept quiet and nodded in agreement, stating that bad manners are worse than having no money. He smiled and suggested it might be a fine time for her to find a place in the bushes from which to observe.

Silently, she crawled out of his pocket and ran under a section of low-hanging branches of a nearby and splendid magnolia, leaving tiny footprints in the morning dew. Under the branches and surrounding the tree, well hidden and discreet, were the animals of last night's graveyard encounter. Mr. Monaghan and Kathleen were there, sitting and whispering quietly to the Kinsleys and Ignatius. Miss Molly and the Landry pigs were exchanging stories about last night's walk home and how frightening it was walking through the streets so late, especially after having been in a graveyard. Last night's meeting had run late and some of the animals had been somewhat nervous about walking home. Some had walked together, or had even spent the night at someone else's barn, since they were coming to the field this morning anyway. Now, in the early morning sunlight and the crisp, dewy air, everyone was quietly laughing about how silly and scared they had been. They even recounted some scary moments, embellishing them since there was no danger now. All in all, even though it was a sober occasion, everyone under the tree was in good spirits, for everyone knew, at least according to all accounts, that Rolly had most likely fled and within the half-hour, the duel would be canceled and William the victor by forfeit. They would all go home, tend to their chores or social obligations and hopefully find time to take a nap.

William and Curtis whispered some inside jokes to each other from time to time, snickered softly and then returned to their statuesque and proper posture, waiting silently for Sir Roland Grahame to appear in the mist. They had just regained composure after an especially funny limerick when they saw a figure riding through the fog, horse and rider as one ominous, black ghost heralding doom.

Miss Molly saw the rider first and bent low to announce the arrival of Rolly's second.

"He has arrived! The second of Sir Roland Grahame has arrived by horse.", she reported with great dignity.

"I wonder what excuse Rolly wrote for him. He probably said the Queen needed him right away or England would fall to the French!", laughed one of the Landry pigs.

"Let us watch and see.", advised Savannah, feeling much more relieved that the second had finally shown; it would all be over in minutes.

The animals all found spots from which they could best see; some under leaves, some under branches and some spying through the taller branches. As everyone looked on, waiting to hear Rolly's feeble, scribed attempt at dignity, their eyes turned white and wide. A loud gasp in unison could be heard, enough to turn Mr. Gilbert's head toward the tree. He looked, saw nothing, not even Molly, for she blended in well with the leaves, shrugged and turned back to the dismounting rider: it was Rolly.

Savannah gasped. How could he be here? Everything had gone so well. What about the plan? Rolly packing? The Gentleman Slayer? Oh, this was just too terrible! The animals shuddered and gasped in soft whispers, making just enough noise to peak the interest of William, Curtis and Rolly. The three men looked to the tree, realized it was nothing and returned their attention to the business at hand. A second rider approached; it was Rolly's second. He dismounted, untied a long wooden box from his saddle and set it on a tree stump, close to William's rapier and box. Sir Roland's second and Mr. Gilbert approached each other, shook hands and inspected the opposing weapons. Upon satisfaction, they shook hands again and turned to their respective weapons. Just as did Sir Roland's second, Mr. Gilbert took William's cloak and laid it over his horse's saddle. He then gently lifted William's rapier out of its velvet slumber. With gloved hands, he kept most of the weight on the hilt, careful to only balance the blade with two fingertips. He turned to his friend, held out the sword William called "Miss Betty" and wished him good luck.

Rolly took his sword, grabbing it abruptly from his second and began practicing some very fine, yet wild *parry-ripostes*. One of the Landry pigs commented that Rolly's shoes were inappropriately high for a duel and that was why he seemed to lack control. Some of the other animals agreed, others just stared ahead, waiting for the duel to commence. Ichabod had offered his cloak to Miss Onyx Treacle, who was trembling as much from the morning chill as anxiety.

William very gingerly took "Miss Betty", bowed slightly to Mr. Gilbert and polished Betty's blade with an elegant swipe of a handkerchief he produced from his lapel. He pivoted on his shiny jackboots and assumed the position of salute, ready to begin. With his weapon held up straight in front of his face and his left hand bent behind his back, he waited patiently for Rolly to assume the same so that they may salute and commence. Of course, Rolly took his time, practicing some lunges and thrusts, and one quick *balestra*, just to show off. Eventually, he came to salute, raised his weapon up in the air and, when the two gentlemen had made eye contact, saluted each other with dramatic sweeps of their swords, whisked down and out to their sides. An eerie *whoosh* echoed across the silent field. Upon salute, they both came *en garde* and the duel began.

"So, Gentleman Slayer, at last we clash steel! Ha-ha!", Rolly produced a quick and ruthless *beat four-riposte*, only to be deflected by William's even quicker *encartata*, stepping quickly to the side to avoid being hit.

"You are fast, my friend,", William admired as the two feigned lunges, encircling each other. "I find myself surprised, what with your great, how shall one say, stature."

William smiled and executed a beautiful *advance-lunge* with a *parry three-riposte*. Rolly backed up just in time to avoid a sword tip in his throat. He recovered, laughed a haughty laugh and flicked William's blade just above the hilt. Rolly's blade hit William's steel sharply with an audible *chink* and William pushed off Rolly's blade tip with a flourishing, upward swipe, pushing both men back to their respective start positions.

"I see even a common man can learn the art of the sword with some competence.", Rolly begrudgingly complimented as he took off his great wide frock coat, switching his weapon from hand to hand as needed. "It appears you studied with a Frenchman. Capable enough gents, but entirely without the refinement of the Italians. Obviously, I studied with the Italians, Mr. Byrd.", emphasizing the title of "Mr.".

It occurred to William that Rolly's coat, as it was thrown to his second, looked like a sail switching directions in the wind. This made him laugh and he felt the need to comment.

"I must compliment you on your tailor, Sir Roland. It is rare one can find a man talented enough to turn nautical fabrics into such fashionable garb.", he circled Rolly one time, flicked the tip of his sword with a sharp *beat five* and demonstrated a perfectly lovely *balestra*, catching Rolly's now exposed blouse and ripping into it a healthy slice.

Rolly was beginning to lose his sense of humor, as he had now ruined a fine blouse and was tiring quickly. While he was a skilled swordsman, he was also generally lethargic and unfit, getting most of his exercise only when he lifted a bottle of wine. Besides, the sharp morning air was beginning to pierce his lungs with every breath.

"I understand from my high-positioned sources that the governor is unhappy with your productivity. It seems you spend all your time either practicing your Greek or dancing.", Rolly attempted a couple of thrusts and grew more tired with each one. "Is that the minuet you are dancing this very moment? Very pretty, Mr. Byrd, very pretty."

To the audience holding their breath under the magnolia tree, William appeared to be completely unaffected. His coat was without soiling of blood or mud, his boots were still fairly shiny and he showed not one black curl out of place. He even took a moment to wipe the small trace of blood from Rolly's scrape off his blade with his glove. He then came *en garde* again and waited, like the true gentleman he was, for Rolly to regain his breath.

"After you, my good Sir.", William taunted, bending forward just a touch and opening his arms wide, sword to the side as if inviting Rolly to take a stab. He did just that. Rolly took the opportunity, egged on to anger by William's cocksure nature and displayed a poorly executed *extended-lunge*, landing a good yard from William's chest.

"Tsk, tsk, tsk. Do you still prefer Italian to French fencing? I would ask for a refund of monies.", William advised as he produced a series of *beats*, one after the other, hitting Rolly's sword with his and backing him all the way up against a tree.

Rolly was breathing so hard that he couldn't come up with a witty retort. His face was becoming more and more red; only a sheer facade of etiquette kept him from screaming in William's face. He was losing and he knew it. He had to regain his composure. He couldn't let this mere, untitled aristocrat beat him. Rolly took a deep breath and with all his might, using the huge hilt of his sword he pushed William backward, positioning himself for a strong and fast lunge at William's throat.

"Aaarrrggghhh!!", Rolly groaned as he used the last of his strength to enact the lunge.

Actually, it was a perfect lunge. The tip of Rolly's sword was aimed directly at William's throat and well on its way. Savannah started to scream; the rest of the animals were transfixed on the action. Even William sensed things had gone wrong. He tried to deflect Rolly's weapon, but missed it entirely by swinging his sword too wide.

"I shall see you have a sufficient funeral, my untitled friend!", Rolly mocked as he headed directly for William's neck ruffles. Then, he tripped.

The comment the Landry pig had made earlier about Rolly's shoes was entirely accurate. As Rolly executed the final steps of his attack, his right heel caught in the grass, twisted his knee and Rolly went down like a racehorse in the mud. His sword flew out of his hand and up into the air, just missing William's head. Rolly skidded from one knee to the other, and with the help of the wet morning grass, continued sliding on his chest until he landed face down in the grass at William's still polished boots. Spitting grass from his mouth, he slowly looked up and glared at William, certain this was somehow his entire fault.

Everyone was silent. The moment was here. Mr. Curtis and Rolly's second waited quietly, ready to assume the eventual duties of a duel's aftermath. The animal contingency waited, breath held collectively. Savannah, Dante and Ichabod all looked at each other, as if there was something they could do. Certainly, they did not want Rolly to win, but no one really wanted Rolly to die just because he had a difference of opinion. Still, this was Rolly's call. He had challenged William and William had accepted. A gentlemen's agreement was a gentlemen's agreement. The duel would end at any moment.

William raised his right elbow, drawing his rapier above his head. The field was still, with only the sound of Rolly's heavy breathing and mild simpering. He closed his eyes tightly, gritted his teeth and awaited the moment of death. William took a deep breath, straightened his back, tossed his head to remove obstructive curls from his face and thrust his sword into its black, leather sheath. Using his other hand, he offered it to Rolly to help him to his feet.

Rolly's eyes were still shut firmly. After what seemed like enough time to have been slain, he thought something had gone wrong. Slowly, he opened one eye and saw William leaning over him, sporting a confident smile. Rolly opened the other eye, mouth agape and skittered backward on his hands and feet, like a crab.

"Wh-wh-what are you doing? Are you toying with me?! You awful, awful man! Just kill me if that is what you intend! Just kill me!", Rolly whined in a high-pitched scream.

"Get up, you silly fool. I am not going to kill you.",
he chided as he still held out his hand.

Rolly hesitantly took his hand and with some effort
on William's part, allowed his rather great frame to be
raised from the dewy grass.

"Did you not know?", William continued, reading
Rolly's expression full of confusion. "This was not a duel
to the death, merely first blood. Quarters given freely.", he
explained, pointing to the bloodied tear in Rolly's blouse.

Of course, this was untrue. William knew this.
Rolly knew this. Moreover, William found, just like many a
quarrel in his world of elitism and high social stature, the
entire situation was frivolous and ridiculous. Nobody
deserved to die over opposing worldviews. William knew
the world to be full of different humans and, while there
was no doubt in his mind that his was the superior point of
view, the existence of these differing ideas, if nothing else,
provided him with excellent debating fodder. Whether
Rolly was a nobleman, North Carolina backwoodsman,
Susquehanna or Chickahominy Indian, William enjoyed
good opposing conversation. Should he remain in
Williamsburg, William would be happy to further debate
the issues of education and knowledge versus commerce
and finances with Sir Roland Grahame.

Chapter XVII

The day was a stunning one. The sky was blue as a robin's
egg. Jonquils and trumpet daffodils announced their
presence vibrantly through the verdant fields of
Williamsburg. Sparrows and robins sang a happy, *"Bonjour
and Good Day!"* to all who would listen. Hither and yon,
the industrious and hungry woodpeckers beat a pleasant
rhythm against the sugar maples and live oaks. It was a
wondrous Williamsburg afternoon.

Savannah adjusted her hat, making certain her new
peacock plumes stood at proper attention in its brim. Her
bodice, a majestic emerald green, embroidered with royal
blue and yellow detail, matched her plumes perfectly.
Looking down, she shook her hips, making certain her
emerald, velvet overskirt fell just right over her petticoats
and pannier hoop. While she was fixing her skirts, she
caught sight of her new slippers. She admired them and
thought what a wonderful friend William was. He had
secretly ordered them for her and they had arrived only this
week on a ship from the Far East. Reportedly, they had
come all the way from China. A magnificent green, they put
the finishing touch on her party ensemble. She was beyond

excited about tonight. Tonight everyone would enjoy a great feast and dancing at her new home.

It took some late night discussions with William, Dante and Ichabod, but she finally made up her mind. For her new home, Savannah chose the huge magnolia that stood majestically just outside the College. Within that tree was an entire network of branches and walkways that suited her purposes just fine. She had chosen for her living quarters, a hole about three-quarters of the way up; it was just large enough to hold the few pieces of furniture she now owned. Mrs. Pritchen had given her Bertam's old four-poster bed, armoire and lowboy. Combined with her two Brewster chairs and a cupboard Mrs. Pritchen called a *kas* (supposedly it had come to her during her Massachusetts years all the way from Amsterdam), her tree house was very posh and cozy, even nicer than a lot of humans' homes. A largish, tapestry rug fit perfectly in the center of the floor and a modest collection of silver and pottery candlesticks kept her home well lit in the darker hours.

Just outside the door, was a wide branch. It was wide enough and flat enough to hold a long trestle table. Attached to the table was a bench on one side and a pole that served as a footrest on the other. This was perfect seating for those crisp spring nights and hot summer days.

It was shaded perfectly by the large magnolia leaves, which kept out the scorching sun of summer, the torrential rain of autumn, the light snow of winter and the peaceful showers of spring. Savannah envisioned many an evening, watching the sunset and enjoying late tea and cakes with friends. Friends, it turned out, would be more than plentiful. Bartholomew's home was just a few branches above Savannah's. He decided to partake in a gentleman's education and Savannah, Dante and Ichabod had all agreed to tutor him in any subject he chose. Between the three of them, they had most of the arts, humanities, sciences and languages covered.

Miss Molly and the Landry pigs were known to graze near the tree and Kathleen Monaghan was thinking about moving into a den that had recently been vacated within the base of this particular tree. Plus, there were plenty of birds and other creatures Savannah had yet to meet, and there were plenty who wanted to meet her. Word had gotten around about her close and personal involvement with the Gentleman Slayer and his latest duel. It was all the town could talk about and she was considered very much in the center of sylvan society.

Everyone was invited tonight. An open invitation had been circulated for any and all to join tonight's festivities: a housewarming and victory party for Savannah and William, respectively. William never did know about Savannah's involvement in the Gentleman Slayer rumor; he figured the whole thing was an uncontrollable exaggeration and that was the end of that. He was happy to attend tonight's soiree. Savannah had very formally invited William to christen her new home with her and their friends. William was well known to never turn down an invitation to a social gathering, he accepted and looked forward to the evening with great anticipation.

Savannah looked at the wee clock that sat on her lowboy, double-checked her wig and hat in the mirror near the door and stepped outside to greet the first of her guests: a family of field mice she heard scurrying up to the front door. Tonight would be fun, she was certain of it.

By nightfall, most of Savannah's guest had arrived and, being the consummate hostess, circulated like a humming bird, making sure each and every attendee was comfortable, well-fed and happy. Below the tree, Dante and Ichabod stood in the cool night air, each leaning on their walking sticks and discussing with Petruchio the finer points of fencing, using last week's, now legendary duel as a talking point. Every now and then, one of them would set down his walking stick, unsheathe his sword and demonstrate his point. Petruchio found this all so dramatic and wished he could take lessons. Ichabod thought Petruchio a bit large for such a refined skill, but agreed to teach him what he could.

Up at the trestle table in the patio area, Kathleen and Ignatius talked about Ireland. Kathleen was born in County Sligo and arrived in Virginia just a year ago. What she didn't know about the Emerald Isle first-hand, her grandfather told her in stories every night. At the other end of the table, Mr. Monaghan and Ignatius' mother, Mrs. Kinsley traded recipes for butternut squash bread and pumpkin pie. Bartholomew and the field mice traded secrets of where to find the best wheat and which merchants were friendly and which were deadly with a broom. Bartholomew was standing on his own two feet, no more crutches and no more bandages. He actually looked quite dapper. His mother had made for him a striking frock coat of violet velvet. His powdered wig even had three violet ribbons, two in front and one in back, to match. His shoes were simple and black, but well polished. Savannah looked at him and thought he would indeed make a fine gentleman mouse.

Savannah surveyed all her guests, so happy that they were all happy. Her mother would be proud of her, hosting such a fine gathering. She was watching the Landry pigs below, telling stories and laughing great snorts, when she heard three familiar voices: William, Mr. Curtis and Monsieur LeVau.

"Good evening, Col. Byrd, Mr. Curtis, M'sieur. LeVau!", she called quietly down the tree, careful not to yell, for ladies did not yell.

"*Bon soir* to you, good hostess!", M'sieur LeVau tipped his hat and bowed as Savannah was making her way down the tree to greet her guest of honor and his friends.

"I am fortunate that all three of my dear new friends have been able to join our party. Are you hungry?", she inquired.

"Actually, my dear, Mrs. Pritchen forced upon us a great meal of Virginia ham and corn cakes. However, I have brought this.", he held out a bottle, black with a faded label. "A gift of a 1665 port wine was delivered to me just this morning. Shall we?", he offered.

"You stay down there, I shall bring down some tankards.", Miss Onyx Treacle offered from one of Savannah's many leafy balconies, finding it the perfect opportunity to 'bump into' Ichabod while downstairs .

"Yes, thank you so much, Onyx.", Savannah thanked her new friend. She and Onyx had already done some shopping in Market Square with Kathleen and had made plans to begin needlepointing a large tapestry together with some of the other ladies about town, including Mrs. Pritchen.

"It shows great manners and kindness for Sir Grahame to send you this gift, Col. Byrd.", Savannah acknowledged the gift tag attached.

"Indeed, Mademoiselle,", M'sieur LeVau added. "It seems he has had a complete change of attitude. I hear he has been very nice to many a gentleman at the Capitol."

"I even heard that he complimented Anthony on his fine selection of Darjeeling this morning.", chimed in Mr. Curtis. "It looks as though he may not be as petulant an associate as we had thought this coming session."

"Cheers to that!", William held up his bottle of port and toasted Gilbert and LeVau's imaginary wine tankards.

"I am so sorry Daniel and Mrs. Pritchen could not attend this evening. Is she feeling better?", Savannah asked with great concern.

"Oh, she is doing far better, far more quickly than one would expect after a fall like that.", William explained. "Daniel is staying with her, helping ready the tavern for next week's coming guests."

"He is a fine young man. Your horses will be in great care, I believe, Monsieur Byrd.", M'sieur LeVau commended.

"I am looking forward to returning to my animals. Daniel, too seems excited about beginning his work as a groom. I imagine he will a fine addition to my staff."

The three gentlemen segued into talk of plantation management, racehorses and some matters of business. Eventually, as one would expect, the discourse turned to lively talk of Greek philosophers and French poets.

What a wonderful evening. What a wonderful start to a new life. Savannah made lifelong friends in William, Dante, Mrs. Pritchen, Bartholomew and even Ichabod, even though he was a bit of a snob. Through something as dreadful as a duel, countless other friendships had been forged. Even Rolly, Savannah stopped and reproached herself, *Sir Roland Grahame*, had somehow morphed from foe to friend. Maybe someday, she would be able to meet Sir Grahame and he would accept her as a friend, and not just a squirrel.

Petruchio even agreed to divide his time betwixt Mrs. Pritchen and Sir Grahame, who had been treating him decidedly better since the duel. She supposed nearly losing one's life and one's dog could make a person think. Could

Sir Roland become a thinking man? Hmm. There was so much to expect, so many things to happen in the coming days. There was her new home, which she loved absolutely; her new friends; and, her new scholarly pursuits. Soon, she would embark on an academic journey of philosophy, law, language and the fine arts. She was excited about resuming her French and violin lessons. She was even more excited about commencing her lecture-and-discussion "classes" with William. Mr. Curtis had offered to tutor her in the fundamentals of Greek law and M. LeVau had offered her lessons in French language and modern French culture. Lost in her own world of academia and the launch into a new life, she was oblivious to the sounds of revelry and merriment surrounding her. As well, she was oblivious to William's appeal for her attention.

"Miss Savannah? Miss Savannah?"

She continued to be self-absorbed.

"My dear? Are you dreaming in a wonderland?", he asked quietly.

Savannah shook her head and focused on William.

"Oh, I am sorry. Just a wee bit lost in my own head.", she apologized. "Are you having a pleasant evening?"

"Quite pleasant. As you know, I enjoy more than anything good friends, good comestibles and good conversation. However, I have promised my presence at a gathering this evening at Governor Nott's home. It is an invitation I cannot ignore. You understand. I shall bid you a good night."

"Of course I understand, he is the governor! Still, I always dread to see a guest depart. Would you like some company on the walk. It has been a few days since I have ridden in your pocket.", she laughed.

"No, no, you stay with your other guests. We will have some breakfast tomorrow morning. I will alert Daniel to one more place setting. You can give Mrs. Pritchen your best in person. I am certain she will be hobbling around the kitchen doing more work than she should.", William remarked. "Before I leave though, I have a housewarming gift for you."

"A gift? For me? How very unnecessary and sweet of you.", Savannah squealed.

She loved presents, but her well-mannered upbringing told her not to appear too anxious about receiving one. While she pretended to be very nonchalant about the surprise, William noticed her eyes darting about his person, searching for packages and bows. He laughed to himself and handed her a small package, wrapped in blue silk and tied with a black ribbon. Savannah tried to take it without seeming too eager. Very delicately, she untied the bow and unwrapped the fabric, trying awfully hard not to show excessive enthusiasm.

"What beautiful ribbon. This will make quite a nice accessory on one of my dresses.", she held it up to her bodice and smiled to herself.

Finally removing the silk, the contents were revealed and she was speechless. It was the most wonderful gift of which she could have dreamed. She looked at William, stunned in gratitude.

"Why, your own copy of Plato's <u>Republic</u>. I. . .I. . .", she stammered, "I know not what to say. This is far too generous. I know how you love this copy. I have seen you reading from it early before breakfast to late before bed. I cannot accept something so dear."

"I want you to have it. It will become your companion in all of your studies. You will find it will aid you in every discipline. As I did, you will find yourself reading it day and night, for Plato and philosophy never grow old, never become overused. He and his work are as important and relevant today as they were two thousand years ago. He taught us how to approach and apply the concepts of thought, government, politics and justice. This book will serve you well throughout your entire life, Miss Savannah. I want you to know Plato.", he said very plainly.

With that, he said, "*Bonne nuit*" and she agreed to join everyone for breakfast in the morning. She waved as he walked into the night, crunching oyster shells beneath his buckled shoes.

By very, very late that evening, all of her guests had departed and Bartholomew had run back to his home. He would be joining them for breakfast, too, as Savannah's guest. He would enjoy William's company and could learn a great deal from such a greatly refined gentleman.

Savannah changed out of her festive garments and donned a simple, white, cotton nightgown and cap. Blowing out all her candles except one, she curled up in her four-poster bed with a cup of Anthony's finest chamomile and looked reverently at the cover of her new copy of The Republic of Plato. It was already very old and well loved. Gingerly, she opened it to the first page and began to read.

" *Chapter I: Cephalus. Justice as Honesty in Word and Deed.*

Socrates: I walked down to the Piraeus yesterday with Glaucon, the son of Ariston, to make my prayers to the goddess. As this was the first celebration of her festival, I wished also to see how the ceremony would be conducted. The Thracians. . ."

Jennifer lives with her best pal and husband, Gary along Virginia's stunning and inspiring Chesapeake Bay. Also there reside their three egregiously precocious pets: two black Tea-cup Pomeranians named Ichabod and Onyx and a black Bombay cat named Catrina, though given the loving moniker of Devil Kitty by her Auntie Kathy. The family spends much of their time between their native home of Orange County, California and their newly-adopted Mid-Atlantic. The historic Williamsburg of this story is also home to Jennifer's parents, Dr. and Mrs. Robert and Pauline Gerstle. Williamsburg rests comfortably between the James and York Rivers.